THE SUICIDE SQUAD

• • • • • • • • • • • • • • • • •

The Pro Book Four

RICHARD CURTIS

WOLFPACK
PUBLISHING
— EST 2013 —

WOLFPACK
PUBLISHING
— EST 2013 —

The Suicide Squad

Paperback Edition
Copyright © 2020 (As Revised) Richard Curtis

Wolfpack Publishing
6032 Wheat Penny Avenue
Las Vegas, NV 89122

wolfpackpublishing.com

Paperback ISBN 978-1-64734-966-0
eBook ISBN 978-1-64734-059-9
Library of Congress Control Number: 2020944892

THE SUICIDE SQUAD

· · · · · · · · · · · · · · · · ·

This is for Jerry and Hester and Matt and Bettiane, and for John Jakes. And a special Order of the Red Dog for Bob Abel.

Chapter I

· · · ·

Trust your agent and God, in that order.

That is Dave Bolt's First Law and it ought to be engraved on the heart of every professional athlete seeking representation. Sure, we players' agents are fallible but our judgment in money matters is infinitely superior to that of most athletes, believe me.

Jimmy Quinn didn't believe me and he paid through the nose.

Jimmy was quarterback of the Indianapolis Racers, then in its second year as a National Football League expansion club. My handsome, rusty-haired, freckle-faced client, a former Ohio State star, had led his team into a place of contention in the Central Division and they were clinging to first place late in the season. He wasn't a spectacular quarterback but he had poise and maturity far beyond his twenty-three years. His specialty was not making mistakes, a skill I'll trade for any three others you can name. He'd been intercepted four times the whole season. He knew how to throw the ball away, eat it, or take a rushing lineman's best shot while getting off a last-moment pass. If he stayed healthy, he was surely destined to become a biggie.

His call came in as I was downing the tail end of a pastrami-rye-light—mustard-hold-the-coleslaw—and a Coke in my office on a Monday afternoon in the third week of November. The Racers were scheduled to go against the Detroit Lions in Indianapolis on Monday Night Football that evening, with the revived second-place Lions bidding for a tie in the standings with the Racers. It was a game I wouldn't have missed for anything and I'd been looking forward all day to settling down in front of a twenty-one-inch screen with some close friends that evening. The last thing I'd have predicted is that I'd be sitting in Racer Stadium watching it live but that's what happened.

Jimmy's call took the form of a screen play. A friendly, open "Hi, Dave. How's things?"

"Hey, Jimmy! Things are just dandy. You up for the game?"

"Higher 'n a satellite. How'd you like to come out here and see us ream the Lions tonight? I can put you in the best seats in the house."

It was tempting but I said, "Much as I'd love to, I've got some pressing appointments early tomorrow morning. I'm afraid I'll have to be a no-show. But I'll be watching—"

"Dave?" His voice had dropped in timbre from happy-go-lucky to grave and here's where he delivered his screen pass. "Dave, I. . . I really need to see you."

"What's the matter, buddy?"

"A problem."

"Why don't you hit me with it over the phone?"

"I really can't."

"Can you give me a hint?"

"Mmm. . . no. No, I really can't."

"Serious?"

"I wouldn't trouble you this way if it wasn't serious. I'll pay your air fare."

"Shit, I don't care about that." I drummed my fingers on the desk and opened my appointment calendar. I was booked solid tomorrow morning—a breakfast with Alvin Dark, a midmorning meeting with Red Auerbach, and lunch with some people from Wilson Sporting Goods to discuss endorsements by some of my clients. Engagements not to be broken lightly. I said as much to Jimmy. As I had a critical and absolutely unbreakable meeting this afternoon, I wouldn't be able to get away until late, so I couldn't see Jimmy before the game. Meaning we'd have to get together afterwards, meaning I couldn't catch a flight back to New York till the following day. "Now, is it that serious, Jimmy?"

"Uh. . . yes," he said, his voice cracking with nervousness.

"Okay, where do you want to get together?"

"There's a restaurant, Barber's, everyone knows where it is. I'll meet you there a little after midnight."

"Unless there's an overtime," I sighed.

"There's not going to be an overtime," he said confidently.

True to his word, Jimmy arranged for me to have the best seats in the newly completed stadium. Located in the second tier on the fifty-yard line, they obviously had been designated by the architect to be the focal point of the bitter winter wind that swept off the prairie and funneled through the open west end of the stadium. Even my forethought in bringing two sweaters, a mouton overcoat, a heavy wool scarf, a knit woolen hat, and a pint flask of Wild Turkey availed little to ward off the vicious chill of the Indiana night. They say that in cold weather a man's scrotum stretches tight in order to bring his balls closer to his warm body. Well, five minutes into the first quarter mine was stretched tighter than the skins on Buddy Rich's drums as my balls sought refuge somewhere in the region of my pancreas.

I will say, though, that the game did some to take my mind off the cold. Both the Lions and the Racers wanted to win something awful and they came out popping. Greg Landry, the Lion's QB and for my money one of the best in the NFL, was never sharper, marching his reconstituted team—there'd been a purge of veterans after their last catastrophic season—up-field from their own twenty-eight-yard line deep into Racer territory on the strength of a purely passing offense which caught the Racers off balance. Not a single ground play did Landry essay until, with third down and five to go on the Racers' eighteen, he called a draw that caught the Racers' middle linebacker, Gene Harvey, on a blitz. The play went for thirteen yards, then Landry, after two fruitless attempts to crack the Racers' line with off-tackle plays, bootlegged the ball into the end zone without a finger being laid on him.

But Jimmy Quinn brought the Racers right back with a ninety-yard march, and, almost as a way of thumbing his nose at Greg Landry, Jimmy picked up most of it in the air. It was mostly nickel-and-dime, slant-ins, square-outs, and buttonhooks for four or five yards at a time, a bruising end-sweep to pick up the first down, then back to aerials. A honey of a screen, with Quinn permitting himself to be chased fifteen yards before unloading to his halfback Enos Jespersen, went for sixteen yards, then Jimmy uncorked a nifty bullet to his tight end Jerry Scorese threading the needle of the Lion's zone defense on a deep slant. The safety brought him down on the five, and on the next play, Jesperson barged through a gantlet of Lion defenders to tumble into the end zone.

"And it looks like we have a game!" Frank Gifford was blaring on a portable television set sitting in the lap of a fan in front of me.

"Indisputably, Giff," affirmed the voice of Guess Who.

"Of course, if I'd been playing on that defensive line," deadpanned former Detroit rushing great Alex Karras, "Jesperson would've got in a lot faster."

"If you're fishing for a compliment," Cosell retorted, "you'll find me taking the bait with alacrity, Alex Karras. If you'd been on that line, I guarantee Jespersen would have been stopped dead in his tracks."

"Shucks, Howard, you're only saying that because I outweigh you by seventy-five pounds," Karras came back.

The rest of the quarter settled into a defensive duel with two exchanges of punts, then Greg Landry found his second wind and took his team seventy yards for a touchdown, forty-five of them on the wings of a perfectly thrown deep sideline pass to a wing-footed rookie wide receiver named Phil Becker. Jimmy Quinn shifted to a ground game after finding a weak spot in the Lions' rushing end but finished a long drive that started on his own six with three gorgeous completions to wide end, tight end, and halfback respectively. And just before the half ended, the Racers advanced far enough into Lion territory to pick up a field goal. Going into the locker room, the Racers held a three-point edge, 17—14.

It took a major effort of will to motivate my muscles to propel me out of my seat. I knew how those Arctic explorers felt when they were tempted to lie down in the midst of a blizzard and lapse into that sweet icy sleep from which there is no awakening. But I managed to pull myself into something of an erect posture and forge my way to a concession stand. I'm not crazy about hot chocolate but at that point, I'd have gladly consumed a quart of pure arsenic as long as it was hot.

I dropped in on Gifford, Cosell, and Karras in the broadcasting booth, pressed flesh, and exchanged pleasantries. Frank was kind enough to arrange for me to sit in an enclosed press box with some ABC station executives who'd also fled from the cold front and I spent the second half in shirtsleeves complaining about the intolerable heat. But at least my game leg (the ankle injury that forced my premature retirement from the Dallas Cowboys acts up in cold, damp weather) thawed out and the prospect of confinement to a wheelchair was postponed for a few years.

The third quarter was a distinct disappointment after the exciting first two. Both teams played sluggishly, and I suspect they'd gotten too comfortable in their warm locker rooms. The Lions nudged a field goal over the crossbars from thirty yards out to tie the score but the period was played entirely between the twenty-five-yard markers and I actually dozed off for a minute, only to find nothing had transpired during my nap. Undoubtedly the respective coaches laid some sharp words on their boys between quarters because when play resumed we were plunged back into the brand of football we'd witnessed in the first half. A Racer interception on Landry woke up the offense and fans alike and Jimmy Quinn came on strong with as pretty a march as you're likely to see, weaving ground and air games into a tapestry of rare loveliness. Racers 24, Lions 17. The Lions didn't come back on their own set of downs but after an exchange of punts, Landry electrified his teammates with a run on a busted play that netted him twenty-five yards and instead of running out of bounds as a prudent quarterback ought to do when a safety is coming up with blood in his eye, Landry lowered his shoulder and bowled the startled player over, reminding me of Joe Kapp in his heyday. Landry then assembled a drive that took the Lions in on six plays. Tie game again.

Then the Lion defense sagged when its capstone, middle linebacker Herb Ryder, got his bell rung and wobbled off the field wondering what year it was. Jimmy Quinn exploited it immediately with a series of slants aimed at befuddling Ryder's rookie replacement. Four plays later, Quinn took the ball in on a sneak, and when the Lions fumbled the kickoff, Quinn shattered the game open like a piñata with a perfectly thrown post pattern to his tight end and that was the ball game.

I traipsed out of the stadium, clinging to the crowd to extract a little extra warmth against the frigid blasts that awaited us outside. Luckily, there was a long line of taxis scooping up fares as fast as customers could jump in. As Jimmy had predicted, the driver knew where Barber's was and drove me to a modern, spacious restaurant on the ground floor of a newly erected skyscraper in midtown about six minutes from the stadium. I waited at the bar for half an hour nursing a Galliano on the rocks, a rare departure from my customary bourbon, but I'd had enough of my customary bourbon for one night and the sweet liqueur soothed my stomach and prepared it for the sumptuous dinner ahead. But after forty-five minutes I began to get a little impatient and a lot hungry and after an hour I began to get worried.

I had no phone number for the Racers' locker room, even assuming Jimmy was still there, so on the off chance he might have gone home for some inexplicable reason, I called there. A female voice answered, sonorous and well-modulated, like an executive secretary's. This would be Jimmy's wife Carol, whom I'd never met.

"Mrs. Quinn?"

"Yes?"

"Dave Bolt."

There was a pause, which I interpreted as confusion.

"Is Jimmy there?" I asked.

"Why, no. Isn't he with you? He said he was meeting you after the game."

"He hasn't arrived yet."

"How odd."

"He didn't call you or anything?"

"No."

"Does he usually loiter around the locker room after a game?"

"Not for an hour. Not when he has an appointment. Look, I have the private number for the locker room. Give me the number you're calling from and I'll call you right back."

I read the number off the phone, hung up, and waited. A trickle of adrenaline accelerated my heartbeat, but I'd been around ballplayers too long to get genuinely concerned.

Genuine concern came a minute later when Carol called back and said Jimmy had left the stadium forty-five minutes ago. And the adrenaline valves really opened when Carol said, "I was afraid something like this was going to happen."

"What does that mean?"

"I'm not sure," she said, voice now trembling with anxiety. "But he's been nervous, uptight, all week. Something's been bothering him and I don't mean worry about the game. In fact, Jimmy doesn't worry about games. This was something else and something important."

"Do you have a clue what it might be?"

"No. Oh, of course. . ."

She censored the thought and I said, "Of course what? It might be a woman?"

"It wouldn't be the first time," she said resignedly.

"Mrs. Quinn, can you come down here now?"

"No, there's no one to watch the kids. But maybe you can come over here. We're only fifteen minutes away from where you are."

She gave me directions and, after leaving word with the maître d' where I was going to be in case Jimmy finally turned up, I hailed a taxi and directed him to a suburb named Beechwood and a street named Alvin Court. The third house on the left was a small ranch house which looked like the first house on the left, the second house on the left the fourth house on the left, the first house on the right, ad suburban. It was just right for the income bracket of a second-year quarterback but if Jimmy carried his team to the playoffs, he'd be looking for larger quarters in the spring. His contract came up for renewal and visions of many digits danced in my head or had until today. They'd been replaced by some chilling fantasies and as I pushed the bell it was all I could do to force a knot of fear back down my gullet. Up to now, I'd been hoping against hope that Jimmy had blown some minor problem out of proportion, a hundred-dollar overdraft at his bank or something. But I knew it was not to be. You just had to be standing there in the middle of a dark Indianapolis suburb at one-thirty in the morning, when all good little quarterbacks are snug in bed with their wives and lights out, to know it was not to be.

It is all but federal law that dashing young quarterbacks must have beautiful wives but I must say I wasn't prepared for the beauty that greeted me at the door. Between her mention of kids and the lateness of the hour when even movie starlets tend to look a little frumpy, I'd expected a woman somewhat on the heavy side in a flannel robe, bunny rabbit slippers, and curlers. Rarely have expectations been so gratifyingly disappointed. Carol Quinn was tall, lithe, soft, and beautiful. She had long brunette hair brushed to a high gloss, framing a face that was faintly Eurasian in bone structure, wide almond eyes, a slightly snubbed nose, generous lips. Her complexion was a beige tint highlighted by a kind of sunrise pink and so smooth it looked as though it had been finished with a jeweler's cloth.

She wore a sand-colored chiffon negligee over a flowing nightgown that invited stares but rewarded them only with the almost imperceptible button outlines of her nipples on small, high breasts, still, a bounteous reward considering what I'd imagined I'd find standing on the other side of the door.

Her mouth was drawn down with worry but she managed a warm smile as she reached out to press my hand, a hand so cold it sent a shiver through her. I realized I was standing stupidly in the doorway and I stepped inside, shuddering.

I removed my coat, scarf, and hat and draped them over a little chair in the hallway, and Carol led me into the living room. Her chiffon swished as she moved and she left a trail of fragrance that elicited naughty fantasies from my brain. The living room was boxy and simply furnished but Carol, apparently, had a nice decorator's touch. The inexpensive colonial furniture, rust-colored carpet, and bright print draperies were sensitively mixed and matched. Despite so many opportunities for vulgarity, Carol had created a warm and comfortable home.

"You look like you could use a drink," she said, gliding to a bar-cart in a corner of the room.

"As a matter of fact, I've used enough drink for one evening, thank you. But if you wouldn't mind putting up some coffee, don't trouble yourself, instant will do just fine. . ."

"Certainly, but if you don't mind. . ." She poured herself a stiffish glass of vodka over a single ice cube. "I haven't had quite enough to drink, myself. Not that I'm a drinker. . ."

"I think you can be excused, considering the circumstances."

She demolished half the glass in one swig without wincing, making me wonder how valid was her protest that she wasn't a drinker. "Will you have a bite to eat, too?" she asked, flowing toward a swinging door that obviously led to the kitchen.

"If it's not too much trouble. I'm kind of. . . well, famished is what I'm kind of." I started for the kitchen, but she waved me off.

"You sit right there. I'll be back in one minute."

I was too jumpy to sit, so I paced the room while Carol tinkered in the kitchen, looking at a little collection of seashells, then at a shelf of books, divided into industrial engineering texts belonging to Jimmy, bestsellers and Book-of-the-Month Club selections for Carol. I halted in front of an antique mirror and grimaced at my own face. Even at the best of times, I grimace at my face, or at least at my poor old nose, a collection of bone-shards no longer than a match head, compliments of high school, college, military, and professional football players and one jealous husband. I keep resolving to have my nose fixed now that I don't play football anymore, but I really can't spare the time, and besides, in the back of my head is the suspicion that I haven't met the last of the jealous husbands.

The rattle of plates on a tray underlined that thought.

I raked my hair with my fingernails, kinky ochre hair that betrays a liaison between an ancestor and a slave girl, which makes me certifiably lynchable in the South, though the hair is the only hint that I'm not of pure Anglo stock, the hair, I should say, and an ineffable compassion for people of the black race.

One last check-out in the mirror, because I felt this inexplicable urge to be as attractive as possible when Carol Quinn came back through the kitchen door. Not bad, not bad, but only hot food and coffee would drain the purple out of my cheeks from the bitterly cold night.

She swept back into the room trailing clouds of glory and bearing a tray laden with meatloaf, a pitcher of gravy, and a mug of coffee steaming tantalizingly. "The meatloaf is cold," she apologized, "but the gravy is warm and the coffee is like lava."

"You're very kind," I said, plunging into the repast while Carol refilled her vodka glass and sipped from it, watching me eat with a kind of Jewish Mother pleasure. I ate fast, not just because I was hungry but also because I wanted to talk. I finished, suppressed a belch, sipped some coffee, and leaned forward in my chair. "Mrs. Quinn—"

"Carol, please." Her dark eyes kindled slightly with the invitation to familiarity.

"Carol. You said that Jimmy was nervous, upset, all week long. You don't know why, what it might be?"

She shook her head, her tresses swirling from shoulder to shoulder in slow motion, like someone in a shampoo commercial. 'Did Jimmy have money problems?" I asked.

"Just the usual, making-ends-meet problems. Actually, come to think of it, he told me not too long ago that we were in good shape. Some kind of investment he'd made had panned out and we have a cushion."

"Did he tell you what that investment was?"

She pulled her legs up under her on the couch opposite me and smoothed her negligee down with graceful hands. "No."

"Now, don't be mad at me, but—did Jimmy ever associate with anyone suspicious? You know, gambler types?"

"I seriously doubt it. He's very. . . um. . . moral about things like that. In fact, he once bawled out a teammate of his for talking too much to a stranger at a bar. No, I can't believe Jimmy would get mixed up in anything like gambling."

Though I broke off that line of questioning, I reserved judgment on Carol's reply. A ballplayer could very well be up to his ears in gambling and his wife wouldn't have a scintilla of suspicion. For the next question, I moderated my voice; it dealt with a subject as delicate as Flemish lace.

"You said something about other women. Do you mind. . . uh. . . elaborating?"

She sighed and lubricated her throat with vodka for the difficult conversation ahead. "There've been other girls, what can I say?"

"Looking at you, I know what I'd say."

She looked at me with appreciation tinged with something volatile and dangerous as if her need for flattery approached desperation. Her ego had been badly bruised and she clutched at my compliment like a floating spar in a shipwreck. "You wouldn't say it if you'd seen me pregnant which I was for eighteen out of the first twenty-two months of our marriage."

"I understand," I said, flashing back to the time when Nancy, now my ex-wife, was pregnant with Jody. For a man with normal sexual appetites, pregnancy is almost as difficult as it is for his wife. Jimmy wouldn't be the first man to have sought relief outside his marriage during that trying period.

"But you're not pregnant now," I said, taking advantage of a natural opportunity to study Carol's soft body directly. She certainly wasn't pregnant except perhaps with a needy sexuality that unnerved me.

"Bite your tongue!" she laughed. "No, I'm not. But Jimmy's tasted the apple. And God knows he has enough girls to choose from. He needs a fullback to run interference for him when he comes out of the locker room."

"All I meant was, now that you're back in good shape—in lovely, lovely shape. . ." It was madness to flirt with her this way but the normal mechanism of restraint seemed to have broken down and the words just rolled out of my throat unchecked.

She ran a hand through her hair seductively and God knows where things would have gone from there had not the phone rang. "There's our boy now," I said with a breeziness I didn't really feel.

"I don't think so," she said, rising in a fluid motion and crossing the room to the telephone on a table beside a rocking chair in the corner. "When I called the locker room, I spoke to Hobie Gilmore. He said he'd call. He wanted to speak to you."

Gilmore was head coach of the Racers, a highly respected and popular man around the league and a hometown Hoosier favorite, as he'd starred for Indiana University and later coached them before becoming an assistant coach with the Houston Oilers. He'd then been tapped for the head coach slot when the NFL awarded a franchise to a syndicate of Indianapolis investors. His popularity was always a puzzle to me; he was a dour, testy man who hated the press, scorned public relations, and disdained anything that did not bear directly on improving his team. But he'd fired the rookie club up from the first minute he took command, sparking them to a winning record the first year and now a place of contention the second and the press accepted his abuse good-naturedly—as long as the Racers won.

Carol picked up the phone and answered it breathlessly, obviously cherishing the slim hope that it was Jimmy. Her shoulders drooped when the caller identified himself and she held the phone out to me.

"Hello, Hobie. Any word on Jimmy?" I said.

"No. You?" His voice was a nasal baritone and he spoke in grunts.

"No. Do you have any ideas?"

"I didn't until half time."

"What happened at half time?"

"You know somebody named Barry Posner?"

"Sounds familiar but I can't place it exactly."

"He's a member of the Commissioner's security staff."

I snapped my fingers. "Right." The Commissioner retains a number of men whose sole duty is to investigate rumors of suspicious activities among pro football players, especially those related to gambling. The nicest thing I've heard football players call them is police but they're a grim necessity and will always be until the Second Coming when mankind is redeemed and made incorruptible.

"Posner collared me outside the locker room," Gilmore said. "He told me tonight's game had been taken off the boards early this afternoon."

"Whoo boy," I groaned. "Taken off the boards" is gambling parlance for calling off all bets. Bookies will stop taking betting action on a game if they have any reason to believe there's something fishy about it. The NFL security boys like this Barry Posner keep their fingers firmly on the pulses of bookies, betting operations, and the people who make up the odds, in order to detect precisely such a flutter.

So much for Carol's confidence that Jimmy couldn't possibly be involved in gambling.

But, of course, this was jumping to conclusions. On the other hand, the connection between Gilmore's news and Jimmy's disappearance was too ominously logical to dismiss lightly.

"Did Posner have any notion as to why?" I asked.

"Yes. He said someone dumped a ton of money on the game, taking Detroit on the point spread."

"What was the spread? Four?"

"Five. We were favored by five."

"Who was it who put the money down, did Posner know?"

"No, he's checking into it now. Whoever it was tried to screen his bet by going through half a dozen front men around the country but rumors started flying and you know how fast rumors fly through the gambling network."

"Faster than a joke," I said. I thought about it for a

moment, fishing for an intelligent question hovering just out of reach. Then it came to me. "Did Posner say exactly when the game was taken off the boards?"

"I told you, he said early this afternoon."

"He wasn't more specific than that?"

"No. Why?"

"Just curious," I fibbed.

Gilmore didn't buy it. "You know something."

"No, honest," I protested.

"Why did you fly out here today? Not just to freeze your ass off watching a football game."

"I have other business out here," I replied casually, seeing no reason to draw Gilmore into the matter at this stage.

"Why don't I believe you?" Gilmore said.

"Oh, ye of little faith! Do me a favor, call me if you learn anything more."

"Where will you be?"

That was a good question. Jimmy had said he'd book an accommodation for me but he didn't say where. I put my hand over the mouthpiece. "Did Jimmy say what hotel he was putting me up in?" I asked Carol.

She looked at me, first levelly, then meaningfully. "It's too late for you to go hunting up a hotel. You can stay here."

I uncupped the mouthpiece, gulping. "Uh, I'm not sure yet. I'll call you tomorrow morning."

"Posner's going to want to speak to you. And we'll have to prepare a story for the press."

"Right."

I put the phone on the receiver and looked at Carol. She was draped on the couch, her dark hair shimmering in the quiet light, her negligee flowing in gentle swirls along the contours of her body. "I don't want to put you to any trouble," I said politely.

"It's no trouble," she said softly. "It's no trouble at all."

Chapter II

• • • •

It may have been no trouble at all for her but for me, the situation reeked of trouble. I have no more compunctions than the next guy about obliging a beautiful, desirable, love-starved, forlorn wife, my justification being that any man who neglects a woman as lovely as Carol has no reason to complain if she accepts overtures from another man. But in this case, the would-be cuckold was my client, ten percent of whose future would pay my office rent and then some and I don't have to tell you what office space rents for in New York. I hate to sound so crass but my daddy's injunction, "Never shit where you eat," had served me well over the years. There are plenty of sex-starved wives around with whom a liaison would cost me nothing. Carol was not one of them; the trouble was, I was in the same room with her and the radiations of desire emitting from her eyes swept over me like gamma rays from a block of pure plutonium.

"I think I'll have that drink now," I said, crossing to the liquor cart.

She handed me her glass as I went past the couch and I refilled it.

"So it's gambling," she said, drawing a quarter of the booze into her throat in one sip.

"It appears to be."

"I can't believe it."

"How well do you know your husband?"

"At least I thought I knew him that well." Her eyes started to mist up and she raised the glass to her mouth. I stayed it with my hand.

"That's not the best way to deal with the problem," I said. "Besides, I need you sober. We've got some work to do."

"What kind of work?"

"I want to go through Jimmy's effects, papers, records, whatever. I'd particularly like to see his bank statements and passbooks, if you know where he keeps them."

"He has a strongbox, but I don't know where the key is."

"Let's look."

"The bedroom is this way," she said, rising a little unsteadily to her feet. I followed her into a hallway off the living room, past a gaily painted door that was obviously the kids' room and into a small, tidy bedroom with a handsome brass bed and authentic Mexican furniture, tastefully decorated and not overly feminine. She went to a tall chest on which stood two football trophies and three game balls Jimmy had been awarded by the Racers over the past couple of seasons, each inscribed in nail polish with the name of the opponents and the score.

Carol opened the top drawers, one containing an assortment of jewelry, collar stays, mementos, and photographs of Carol and the kids, a stocky little boy and a precious little girl, the other contained socks and handkerchiefs. Carol probed through these while I poked through some objects, miniature trophies, geodes, and other sentimental junk, on the night table on Jimmy's side of the bed. Carol went through the rest of the drawers in the chest then I ransacked the pockets of his suits and pants in the wardrobe.

"Nothing here," she said.

"Me neither. Where's that strongbox?"

"Under the bed."

I kneeled down and slipped my hand under the dust ruffle and found the leather handle of a small metal box. It was a cheap brand with a simple lock. I called for a screwdriver and two minutes of prying sprang it.

Inside the box was an accordion file with each category marked neatly on tabs—Insurance, Mortgage, Birth Certificates, Medical, Football Contract, Stocks and Bonds.

I reached into the latter pocket and pulled out a thin sheaf of certificates. Five shares of U.S. Steel, five of General Motors, one share of AT&T, six or seven U.S. Savings Bonds of small denomination—a modest portfolio and one in keeping with Jimmy's income bracket. It wasn't what I found that interested me, however, but what I didn't find. I looked up at Carol. "I'd have thought there might be something here relating to that investment you mentioned."

"Maybe it's under 'I' for Investments."

"There's nothing under 'I' except Income Tax Returns." That gave me an idea, and I pulled out a copy of Jimmy's return for last year. My eyes roved down to the heading of Income, but other than his Racer salary, salary received from an engineering firm Jimmy worked for in the off-season, and some stock dividends and savings interest, there was nothing remarkable. Nor did the Capital Gains section show anything particularly interesting. I looked up at Carol again. "When did Jimmy say he'd made that investment?"

She looked at the ceiling and pondered a moment. "Oh, maybe five, six months ago." That would be April or May.

I threw the return back into the file. "Then it wouldn't appear on last year's return but on next April's, assuming he reports it."

She looked at me with a fisheye. "What does that mean?"

"Well, technically speaking, gambling winnings are supposed to be reported. . ."

"Of course," she said dourly.

I ran my fingers over the pleats of the file and stopped at a pocket designated Bank Statements. I reached in and scooped out a thick collection of envelopes held together with a rubber band. These were checking account statements issued by the First National Bank of Indiana. The prospect of going through Jimmy's canceled checks thrilled me not at all and I set them aside for another dip into that pocket. I came up with three savings passbooks, all stamped with the insignia of the Indianapolis Savings and Loan Association. The first belonged to a joint account held by James and Carol Quinn and showed a balance of $1,875.68 with no extraordinary deposits or withdrawals. The second was James and Carol Quinn in Trust for Theodore Blake Quinn and Emily Elizabeth Quinn. A balance of nine hundred dollars and no action save fairly regular deposits of ten or twenty dollars.

"Teddy and Emily are the kids," Carol explained, looking over my shoulder.

"I gathered."

I opened the third passbook, in the name of James Quinn, and sucked my breath in. "Bingo!"

Carol kneeled down beside me. "I didn't know Jimmy had a savings account of his own."

"He does and look at the action."

He had opened the account in February of this year with a two-thousand-dollar deposit. A month later he'd withdrawn a thousand of it and two weeks later deposited three thousand. Two weeks after that, he'd withdrawn twenty-five hundred and a month later deposited ten thousand. Early in May, he'd withdrawn the ten thousand and late in June, he'd put back twenty-five thousand.

Finally, in late September, he'd withdrawn the twenty-five thousand. It had not yet come back to roost but at the geometric scale his deposits had been growing, the next sum he deposited could be close to six digits. Carol gaped at the book, rose shakily to her feet, and plopped down heavily on the edge of the bed. "What does this mean?"

"I hope it means he has a smart stockbroker but I doubt it. There are no papers in the box pertaining to investments of this size. I wonder. . ."

"What do you wonder?"

"Never mind."

She touched my arm. "Dave, please—don't spare my feelings. I've got to know."

I looked at her. Her jaw was set sternly, and she was dry-eyed. It was a judgment call as to whether she could take it. I decided she could. Well, okay. I was wondering if these sums represent payoffs."

"Payoffs for what?"

I gulped before I answered. "Payoffs to throw games or shave points."

She took a long shuddering breath and for a moment I thought she wasn't going to make it. To help her, I quickly added, "But of course, I rule that out."

"You do?" she said immediately, hope flaring explosively in her almond eyes.

"Yes. You see, most of the turnover in this passbook takes place off-season. You don't take money in the spring to throw a football game in the fall. Another thing is, an athlete throwing a game wouldn't take money out of the bank. He'd just put money in. The way this book is structured, Jimmy seems to have been spending money to make money."

"Then you think it could be a legitimate investment," Carol said silently pleading with me to say yes.

I did say yes and I should have put conviction behind it, but I really didn't believe it and it showed. Carol shut her eyes, her face turned scarlet and when she opened her lids tears sluiced out of them and streamed down those alabaster cheeks. I reached out to take her hand, but the rest of her body came with it. She fell into my arms sobbing. I held her tightly, caressing the back of her head and murmuring the futile things one murmurs in these awkward situations.

"Mommy?"

The tiny voice coming from the bedroom doorway startled me like a pistol shot. Carol pushed away abruptly, sniffed, and wiped her nose with the sleeve of her negligee. Two red-haired urchins cuter than bunnies stood staring at us in their Doctor Dentons. Carol rushed to them and put her arms around them. "Why are you crying?" asked the boy, the older of the two.

"Uh, I hurt myself," Carol said.

"Is it bleeding?" the little girl asked.

"No, it's fine now."

"Who's that?" asked Teddy, pointing at me and sliding shyly behind his mother's legs.

"That's Daddy's friend, Uncle Dave."

"Can we have cookies now?" asked Emily.

Carol smiled and hustled them out of the room. "I'll be right back—just want to put them back to bed."

"Good night, Uncle Dave," the kids shouted.

"Don't let the bedbugs bite," I said.

I sat down on the edge of the bed and opened the passbook again, gazing at it as if some invisible message would somehow materialize on the page. That's when I noticed the paper clip. It was fixed to the back cover of the passbook and held a small piece of lined notepaper. On the paper was a list of ten or twelve sets of initials. Opposite each set was a dollar figure, the denominations running from $3,000 to $10,000. I did a rough tally and the total came to something like $85,000.

"Lordy, Lordy," I muttered, staring at the list and trying to make sense out of it. Clearly, the initials represented the names of Jimmy's cohorts in what, for the time being, I would continue to call an "investment scheme," though many a less euphemistic phrase offered itself to mind.

With Carol crooning a lullaby to her children for background music, I ticked off the initials, seeking correspondence between them and people with whom Jimmy might be involved. The obvious association that sprang to mind was football players, and indeed, two sets of initials, B. B. and S. T., might belong to Jimmy's teammates, defensive tackle Bucky Bradley and a second-string wide receiver, Saul Talcott. But then one other B. B. came to mind, Buddy Belindez of the Saints, and two other S. T.'s, Sam Tingley of Philadelphia and Sonny Thomas of San Francisco. I knew a baseball player whose initials were B. B., and a client of mine on the Detroit Pistons basketball club was an S. T. And for all I knew, the initials might belong to the Harvard lacrosse team, the board of directors of the Chase Manhattan Bank, or the kids at the check-out counter of the local A & P. So much for that theory.

Nevertheless, the possibility that these were football players clung to my mind and my heart pounded heavily with the dread that Jimmy was mixed up with a gambling operation involving other players. And there was something about the pattern of withdrawals and deposits in his passbook, the ever-increasing sums, that pointed to a relentlessly growing involvement as if he'd started small just to get his feet wet, then, having tasted success, plunged deeper and deeper into a commitment. At some stage, perhaps this latest one, he had finally drawn other players into it as well. Most ominous of all, if one read between the lines of those balances, was the—how can I put it?—the guaranties of the money. It was as if, having received a three-thousand-dollar return on a thousand-dollar investment the first time, he was able to put up larger sums with complete confidence that the returns would be equally impressive. A cautious man, having banked twenty-five grand after a streak of successful investments, might hedge his bets thereafter by putting up maybe five or ten grand at a time and leaving the rest in the bank. But not Jimmy. He seemed to be absolutely certain of doubling or tripling his money.

There is only one way you can gamble with such complete confidence, there's got to be a fix.

And if the story I read in Jimmy's passbook was true, I was holding in my hand a document of frightening power.

I gazed at it in a semi-stupor, dimly aware of the sound of the bathroom door closing, water running, the sound of the bathroom door closing, water running, the bathroom door opening again. Carol flowed into the room, her eyes clear once again, her skin bright and slightly flushed, as if recently rubbed with a towel. She'd freshened up and was once more the woman who had greeted me at the door.

"I'm sorry," she said, touching me on the arm. "I shouldn't have gone to pieces that way."

"Hell, you've had some rough weather. Can't blame you one little bit." I handed her the passbook and the list, hoping it wouldn't set her off on another crying jag. But she studied the list with composure, looked at me, and shrugged. When I asked her who the initials might belong to, she played back a close copy of my own speculations.

"Whatever it means, this thing is getting more and more sordid," she added, shaking her head.

"Carol, I'd like to hold onto this book and the list, if you don't mind."

"Yes, certainly, I want you to have it." She fell on the bed wearily. "I don't care anymore."

"Don't care about what?"

"If Jimmy's into something wrong, I'm not going to defend him. Do what you have to do. I'm up to anything they can throw at me."

"You just need a good night's sleep. Besides, I'm not convinced Jimmy's into anything wrong. It just looks that way."

She reached up and caressed my chest. "You're just being kind to me."

"Kindness is my middle name."

"Won't you perform one more act of kindness?"

Her fingers traced a line down my chest and over my stomach, then touched a vital organ. I sat over her transfixed as her deft and love-hungry hand began to work me into a frenzy. I reached out and touched her breast. She closed her eyes, pouted, and shuddered. Her legs parted slightly. It would have been so easy.

I got to my feet. "I'm not sure it would be an act of kindness," I said, standing not quite as straight as I might with the painful bulge between my legs.

She looked at me with the eyes of a wounded doe. "Oh, Dave, please. . ."

"I still owe your husband something, even if you don't."

"Dave. . ." She ran her hands up her legs, hiking her negligee and nightgown up her thighs and over her hips. I stood gaping at her nakedness, the temptation singing madly in my head like the fatal song of a siren.

I shut my eyes until the singing subsided. Eyes still closed, I said, "Let's just leave it at 'Uncle Dave' for the time being. I'll sleep on the couch."

I turned and hobbled into the living room.

Chapter III

· · · ·

Consciousness came in the form of the pungent smell of freshly brewed coffee and frying bacon, and four beady eyes staring at me an inch from my nose. "A giraffe was in our room," Emily announced. "But it didn't bite anybody."

"They only go after elephants," I murmured through gunk-clogged lips.

"Uncle Dave, will you fix my Push-Button Farm?" asked Teddy. "The cow doesn't come out."

"Can I at least go to the bathroom and wash my face?"

"No," came the forthright answer.

"Children!" came Carol's scolding voice. "I told you to let Uncle Dave sleep."

"That's all right," I said, unbending and sitting up. "I wanted to be woken up at. . ." I looked at my watch. "Well, maybe not six-thirty. Maybe eleven is when I wanted to be woken up."

Carol came in and shooed the kids into the dinette. She wore a sensible flannel robe and looked slightly disheveled the way another man's wife should look when you're alone in the house with her.

"You can use Jimmy's razor," she said softly, looking at me neutrally.

"I don't trust myself with a razor at this hour," I said.

I wobbled to the bathroom, took a leak and shaved, and emerged still groggy, a condition that would quickly dissolve in strong coffee. "Obviously, you don't have children," Carol said, pouring the delicious ichor into a tall mug. "I've watched the sun come up every day for the past four years."

"I did have one," I said between scalding sips. "I mean, I still do, but she's with my ex-wife down in Fort Worth."

"Ah, sorry. That was tactless."

"That's all right. Nobody's tact glands start pumping until nine in the morning, at least. I don't mind talking about it anyway, at least today. Some days it pains me less than others, if you know what I mean." I told her about how I started drinking after my football injury put me out for the rest of my third season at Dallas, setting me on a course of self-destruction that ended with a promising football career and a marriage in ruins. If it hadn't been for my best friend, a reporter named Roy Lescade (now a sports columnist with the New York Post), who tracked me from bar to bar across the west and finally rescued and rehabilitated me, I'd have been buried ages ago in some potters' field with only a half-filled bourbon bottle to escort me into the netherworld. Roy swung a job for me in the Dallas Cowboys' front office, from which I departed in due time to start my agency. "The rest is just the boring story of my meteoric rise to preeminence in my field," I said, doing a fair imitation of Howard Cosell.

Carol reached out and covered my hand gently. "About last night. . ."

"I behaved like a cad," I grinned, dismissing the matter.

"Will you fix my cow now?" Teddy pleaded.

"Sure. Where's the barn?"

"Play with them a few minutes while I get dressed," Carol requested, "then we'll have a leisurely breakfast."

Repairing Teddy's cow was no sweat but changing the diaper on Emily's Baby Alive took some doing. Presently Carol appeared, dressed prettily in skirt and sweater and scarf, looking slightly ravaged around the eyes but otherwise composed, and sicced the kids off me. While they massacred each other in their room to the strains of a Sesame Street record, Carol and I dined on bacon and eggs and English muffins, exchanging confidences as intimately as if we were lovers. Looking back, I could have kicked myself for not having taken advantage of her. Most of the time, I take pride in my sense of honor but on this occasion, I felt just downright stupid.

We passed the time till around eight-thirty when I phoned Hobie Gilmore and made an appointment to see him and the Commissioner's man, Barry Posner, in the Racers' headquarters in downtown Indianapolis in half an hour. Carol got the kids dressed and we piled into the station wagon. "I'm not going to tell them about this," I said, patting the pocket of my blazer in which resided Jimmy's passbook. "And if anyone asks you, you don't know nothin'. I don't expect the press to bother you today but unless Jimmy shows up by the end of the day, he'll be conspicuously absent from practice tomorrow and we'll have to give out a release explaining why. That's one of the things I'll be discussing with Hobie and Posner this morning and I'll call you to tell you the story we finally settle on. You'll be called for confirmation by reporters but if you play it cool and stick to the story, you'll keep the breath of scandal away from your door. At least, for a while."

We got slightly jammed in rush-hour traffic but finally squirted out of it and into the broad avenue on which the

Commercial Exchange Building, a handsome stone structure
of 1930s vintage, stood and in which the executive offices
of the Indianapolis Racers were housed. I tickled the kids
goodbye and leaned over for a kiss on Carol's check. "Perhaps we'll take a rain check," she murmured in my ear.

"I'll do a Hopi rain dance the second I get out of the
car," I said.

And I did, to the infinite amusement of Teddy and Emily and the shock of workers swarming into the building.

The Racers' offices were on the fifteenth floor, flamboy-
antly decorated in the red, white, and green of the team's
jerseys and with a huge reproduction of the Indy racing car
with footballs for wheels, the team's insignia, on a wall
plaque in the reception room.

A luscious redhead with footballs for tits ushered
me immediately into Hobie Gilmore's office, a simply
furnished, no-nonsense room that reflected its occupant.
Gilmore, a tall, lanky man, greeted me with a strong handshake and introduced me to two other men in the room.
One was Arthur Spartling, owner of the team, a heavyset
man with thinning brown hair who wore an expensive wool
suit and a harried look on his jowly face. I'd spoken to him
a number of times on the phone but never met him.

The other was Barry Posner, the Commissioner's im-
perial envoy, a slight fellow in three-piece serge suit and
dark silk tie. With horn-rimmed glasses, he looked like a
Wall Street account executive but his grip was firm and his
voice, when he greeted me, sharp and commanding. I'd have
expected no less from anyone serving the Czar of Football.

Spartling gestured at a coffee urn in a corner of the room
but I was slightly coffee-logged and held up my palm. I
uttered a chatty congratulation on last night's game, just
to break the ice, but it scarcely chipped the surface, and

Barry Posner launched into business like Terry Metcalf hitting the line on an off-tackle slant.

"Mr. Bolt, Hobie tells me you flew here yesterday specifically to see Jimmy Quinn."

"I don't know where he got that idea," I said. "Like I told him last night, I have business out here and thought I'd take in the game."

"What sort of business?"

I looked squarely into Posner's hostile, arrogant eyes, dilated by his thick glasses, and said, "Mine."

"What sort of business might it be that caused you to abruptly cancel three appointments scheduled for today?"

I laughed nervously and shook my head. "Big Brother strikes again."

"You really ought to play ball with him, Dave," said Spartling. "Whatever you know, he's going to find out anyway."

I sighed and shrugged. "You're absolutely right, Mr. Spartling. It's just that I want to protect my client until there's positive evidence of wrongdoing."

"We all want to do that," Spartling said.

"Christ knows we do," muttered Hobie, lighting a new Marlboro with the burning stub of an old one.

"Okay. Jimmy called me around lunchtime yesterday—"

"Precisely when?" demanded Posner, martinet-like.

I looked at my watch, an idiotic gesture, as if it had stopped at the exact moment Jimmy had called me. "I'd say, one-thirty, a quarter of two, something like that."

"That would be twelve-thirty, a quarter of one, Indianapolis time," Spartling observed. "The game was dropped off the boards just after noon."

Posner looked at him condescendingly, as if that kind of detective work was kid stuff. Looking back at me, he said, "What did Jimmy say to you?"

"He said he had a problem, a serious problem. He couldn't discuss it on the phone and would I please fly out there—here—right away."

"Did you see him before the game?"

"No, I couldn't get away till late in the afternoon—as I'm sure your inquiries will confirm," I said ironically.

"They already have," he said, even more ironically. "Did you speak to him after the game?"

"No, just waited around this restaurant, Barber's, until I got worried and called Jimmy's wife Carol."

"Did she sound surprised to know Jimmy wasn't with you?"

"Floored. She was, and still is, extremely distraught."

"You then went out to see her?"

"Yes. I asked her if she could tell me anything that could explain Jimmy's behavior and disappearance."

"And she said. . .?"

"Only that Jimmy has been extremely nervous all week long."

"That could have been about the game," Spartling interjected.

"No way," Hobie Gilmore replied. "Jimmy was Mister Cool himself, you know that, Mr. Spartling."

"I suppose," the club owner said, burying several chins in the palm of his hand.

"Carol Quinn told you nothing we might find useful?" Posner pressed.

"No, but feel free to ask her yourself," I said.

"I'm grateful for your permission," Posner said unctuously. This was not a lovable man, and as much as I stand in awe of the Commissioner, I determined then and there that nothing less than thumbscrews would make me reveal to Posner what I had discovered in Jimmy's strongbox the night before.

I looked at him. "Do you mind if I ask you a question?"

He obviously did and answered me with a look of scorn.

"Were you able to find out who dumped all that betting action on the Lions yesterday?" I asked, scornful look or not.

"No, not yet," he said. "But I will."

"Would you mind if I tried myself?"

He processed the question through his computer brain, and his eyes flickered only a moment before he spewed forth a readout. "Yes, I think I would."

"Thank you for denying me permission," I said. "But I think I'll try anyway."

"I'll have to report that to the Commissioner."

"You do that, sonny-boy."

Spartling stepped verbally between us. "We're supposed to discuss a press release, gentlemen."

"Why don't we just say Jimmy wrenched his shoulder last night and is in seclusion recuperating," proposed Hobie.

"Sounds good to me," Spartling said.

I agreed.

"I'll have to check with New York," Posner said. Then, looking at me: "I think that's all we have to discuss, Bolt. But if you insist on conducting your own investigation, I trust you'll report any findings to me immediately."

"That's a possibility," I said.

"Dave, please, let's not let personalities get in the way," Spartling begged.

"I'm only doing my job," said Posner.

"Where have I heard that line before?" I mused saluting Spartling and Gilmore and making my exit.

Chapter IV

• • • •

Not only is it not hard to find a bookie in any large city, it's actually easier than finding a policeman. In this case, I had to travel no farther than fifteen floors by elevator to find one. When I emerged on the ground floor of the Commercial Exchange Building, I walked up to the elevator starter, a wizened old dude in a blue uniform four sizes too large, and said, "What's the line on the Green Bay game Sunday?" Half the starters I know take betting action.

He looked at me with faint suspicion since I was a stranger to him, then shrugged. "I heard it was Chicago by three."

"Where can I get down?"

"I'll be glad to oblige you myself, mister. What'd you have in mind?"

"I'll lay ten."

"Ten dollars," he repeated.

"Ten large."

He blanched. "Ten large! Mister, I'm just a little guy. Ten large is ninety-nine hundred dollars more than I ever handle."

"I'm a stranger around here. I don't know anyone."

"I can see that!" he chuckled. "Look, there's a bar on

Chestnut Street, corner of Parmentier, the Five Leaf Clover." He looked at his watch. "It should be open by now. The bartender's name is Howie. He's the man to see for the kind of action you're looking for."

"Thanks, pal."

"Tell him Murray sent you."

"Thanks, Murray," I said, shaking his hand. Mysteriously, a folded ten-dollar bill that had been in my palm when we shook hands had somehow adhered to his.

I found my way to the Five Leaf Clover, a classier-than-average bar about six blocks west of the Commercial Exchange Building. A tall, bulky man stood behind the bar stowing glasses in a rack over his head. He had an enormous paunch, suggesting he drank almost as much beer as he served.

I sat down on a stool in front of him. "Would you be Howie?"

"I would, my friend. What's your pleasure?"

"Murray told me you could help me."

"Ah. Then the drink's on me."

"Thanks but drinking before one in the afternoon is against my religion."

"Suit yourself."

"I need some information."

"I'm a fountain of information," he said openly, testing the soda, water, and beer taps.

"I want to know why last night's game was taken off the boards."

A shadow came over his face. "Sorry, that spigot isn't working."

"I heard that somebody went in for a bundle."

He bit his lip reflectively, then said, "That's common knowledge. It doesn't cost me anything to tell you you heard correct."

"What does it cost you to tell me who the party was?"

"It could cost me my life, Mac."

I took my billfold out of my jacket and laid it on the bar. "How much is your life worth?"

He gazed at the billfold, then at me. "Who you working for?"

"Would you believe me if I told you?"

"No."

I opened my billfold and removed a century note from the little wad of eight or ten I usually carry for a variety of corrupt purposes.

Howie looked at the bill, ambled to the end of the bar, scooped something out of a bowl, returned, and dropped a handful on the hundred-dollar bill.

Peanuts.

I got the message and dropped two more bills on the bar. Howie looked at me patiently and I added still another two, bringing the total to five hundred dollars. He reached out for the money and I enclosed his wrist in an iron grip. "First, the information."

"Well, it's only a rumor, you understand. But I heard it was Al Negri."

"And who might Al Negri be?"

"You're not from around here, are you?"

"No."

"Al Negri is a gambler."

"You've just earned a dollar-fifty. You'll have to be a little more specific to earn the rest."

"He's a lieutenant in a very big gambling syndicate."

"Run by who?"

"Run by a guy named Sammy Wisniak. Wisniak has a big furniture store on the east side of the city. Upstairs, he conducts his. . . uh. . . betting concern."

"Can I find Negri there?"

"Sometimes, but Negri conducts a lot of business from his home. This is his address," he said, scribbling it down on the back of a cardboard beer coaster. "And this is Wisniak's."

"I'll try that one first," I said.

"Just like that?" said Howie, slightly horrified. "You're just gonna walk in and start asking questions?"

"Can you think of a better way?"

"It depends on how high survival is in your priority system."

"I'll take my chances," I said, releasing his wrist. He clutched my money and stuffed it in his apron pocket. I headed for the door, then turned around. "Tell me, Howie, how long will you wait to alert Wisniak after I leave here?"

"About thirty seconds."

"Why so long?"

"I got to take a leak first. Who shall I tell him is on his way?"

"Tell him Dave Bolt."

"I'll watch for the name in the obits," he shouted as I pushed through the door.

As I'd suspected, Wisniak's was a shylock operation parading as a furniture store. It sold schlock stuff at usurious interest rates to poor people, mainly blacks, then harassed them for their money, confiscated their furniture, even put liens on their income. And, of course, on the second floor was a bookmaking operation parading as the second floor of a furniture store.

In my mouton coat and expensive tooled boots and with that kinky blond hair, I wasn't exactly impossible to spot walking in the door and a rather unsavory salesman in a stained silver suit called out my name. He bade me follow him and led me to a freight elevator in the back of the store. "You mind turning around and facing the wall, Mr. Bolt?" he said, leaving me no doubt that I had no choice. "I'll have to check you for weapons."

I shrugged and spread-eagled against the metal wall of the elevator while he frisked me. Then he released me, closed the elevator door, and took her up one floor.

The vista was one of a vast sea of shoddy bedroom suites in mock-Mediterranean, mock-Danish, mock-Louis Quinze, mock-Regency—any style of which mockery was made, they had it. My cicerone escorted me through a maze of king-sized beds, night tables, chests, and wardrobes to a room marked Private No Admittance in large, threatening-red letters. He knocked twice, a bolt was thrown, and the door was opened by a black man of considerable magnitude wearing dark slacks and a black turtleneck sweater. I stepped into a little anteroom with two desks, one of which was occupied by a surprisingly young and handsome dark-completed man in a tasteful business suit. He was on the phone arguing with a manufacturer about delivery dates on a shipment of living room furniture and were it not for the perpetual ringing of telephones filtering through a door behind him, I'd have had no reason to believe this was anything other than what it seemed, the business office of a furniture store.

The handsome man, who I was certain was Wisniak, hung up and leaned back in his swivel chair, looking at me curiously. His eyes were hazel and gentle and the voice with which he uttered my name was mellifluous. I had been prepared for anything but a gentleman and for some reason I got nervous. The most treacherous men I'd dealt with were the baby-faced ones.

"I understand you've been making inquiries about me," he said, picking up a felt-tip pen and doodling figures on a scratchpad. "Exactly whom do you represent?"

His proper use of the pronoun unsettled me even more. I think this was the first bookmaker I'd ever met who was even dimly aware the word "whom" existed and I mused what would happen if the term caught on. "Hey, whom do you like in the sixth at Aqueduct? Whom do you pick in the Knicks game tonight?"

"I represent Jimmy Quinn. I'm his agent."

He absorbed this information with a nod. "How may I help you, Mr. Bolt?"

"I understand last night's game was taken off the boards yesterday. I'm trying to find out why." I held back that Jimmy had disappeared, a piece of information worth a gold mine to a bookmaker, assuming Wisniak didn't know it already.

I'd been prepared for the possibility that Wisniak would look at me blankly and say he hadn't the faintest idea what I was talking about. But apparently, his gambling operation was so well protected that he could talk with impunity. "It was taken off the boards because a gambler who believed he had a sure thing was indiscreet enough to bet a huge amount of money on the game and he scared all the fish out of the pond."

"Was that gambler's name Al Negri?" I asked, holding my breath. I could feel the cruel eyes of the titanic black bodyguard boring into my spine. Wisniak's own eyes, however, were fawnlike, which may be an inappropriate image since fawns are warm-blooded creatures. I was beginning to think Wisniak's blood circulated at something approaching Absolute Zero on the Kelvin scale.

"I really don't know," he said. "I've been trying to find out, but have had no success." He doodled some more on his pad and added, "I don't think it could have been Negri, however."

Now he was using "however." "Why not?" I asked.

"Because Negri works for me and he wouldn't do something like that without my specific authorization."

"But suppose he saw an opportunity to make a killing on his own, without having to cut you in?"

"That would be disloyal," he said so matter-of-factly that to call it an understatement would be an overstatement. With every word Wisniak uttered, I realized more certainly that this was a man with tremendous leverage, a man whose minutest words and actions moved a great many men a great distance. In his mouth, "disloyal" could be the equivalent of a royal dictum of banishment or worse. I would not like to be called disloyal by Sam Wisniak.

"Let me ask you a question, Mr. Bolt," he said. "Do I understand that you're trying to ascertain a possible connection between the removal of last night's game from the boards and your client?"

"Yes, that's right."

He pursed his lips and nodded subtly. "Very interesting, very interesting."

His "Very interesting" was very interesting to me. It seemed to indicate that until this moment, he had not known what was the sure thing on which Negri—or whoever the gambler was—had unloaded so much money. In other words, in going to Wisniak, I'd been barking up the wrong tree.

Al Negri was the man to speak to next.

Wisniak rose from his desk and offered his hand. "Well, Mr. Bolt, I'm afraid I can't be of much help to you. But if I may offer you some good advice, I'd suggest you'd be well off not concerning yourself with the matter any further."

"I can't remember when I've been so agreeably told to mind my own business," I said, shaking his hand.

"I don't tell people what to do, I just make suggestions," he said nodding almost imperceptibly to his bodyguard. "Midge, please show Mr. Bolt out."

"I suppose 'Midge' is short for 'Midget,'" I said to this veritable oak tree of a man as we stepped aboard the elevator.

"Thass right," he said, pushing the button. I watched his hand as he did so. It pressed "B," not "1," meaning he was taking me to the basement. There were only two possible reasons why he was doing that, one of which was to show me some bargains in patio and lawn furniture. The other was to emphasize by means of corporal punishment Sam Wisniak's suggestion that I concern myself no further with the matter of last night's game. I didn't hesitate a second.

I balled my fist and slugged him in the jaw with a ground-floor-up roundhouse right.

It dislocated his jaw, I was sure, and the impact drove his head against the steel wall of the elevator, probably concussing him. Had he been of merely mortal strength and stature, that would have been enough to put him away. But after a second in which his eyes rolled around his face, he charged at me, swinging wildly with both fists like an enraged grizzly. I managed to block the first two but a third attempt with his left struck my kidney and I could hear my own moan as the wind rushed out of my lungs. Dropping my guard for that instant, I opened my own face to a right cross but I jerked my head away and it glanced off my forehead. It didn't hurt at the time but later it swelled up like a pineal eye trying to be born on my brow. I assayed a kick in his nuts but he caught my knee between his thighs and embraced me in a bear hug. My vertebrae clicked from the nape of my neck to the coccyx and a moment later would have snapped had I not used the only weapon I had free, my head, to butt him in his already busted jaw. He grunted and relaxed just enough for me to complete the upthrust of my knee. He released completely and fell away. I made a hammer out of my right fist again and brained him on the temple as he slumped down.

Panting and trembling, I stood over his body, then pushed the second-floor button. The elevator crawled upward and the door opened. I hefted Midge over my shoulder, staggered out, and dumped him on a queen-size bed with a mock-Colonial headboard. Then I got back in the elevator, went to the first floor, and walked out of the building, heeling slightly to starboard to favor my right kidney. I ducked into a coffee shop and went to their men's room. I took a leak with my eyes shut tight; I didn't want to see the blood in my urine.

I dashed some water on my face, wincing at the ugly red egg on my forehead, then reached into my pocket and examined the beer coaster on which Howie the bartender had written Al Negri's address. It was on Biltmore Street in something called the Biltmore Apartments. The cashier in the coffee shop said it was a taxi ride away.

I nailed down a cab and seven or eight minutes later was deposited in front of a huge glass-and-brick rabbit warren surrounded by tonsured lawns, gardens, a fountain and a playground, none of which interested me as much as the police car parked beneath the sweeping port-cochere that fronted the building. Don't ask me what instinct told me it had a bearing on events of the last twenty-four hours, I just knew, that's all.

A bushy-haired kid in a tight doorman's uniform stood smoking a cigarette behind a kind of rostrum with a tenants list on it. "All visitors have to be announced," he stated officiously.

"Mr. Negri?"

His lips parted in a creepy leer. "You can see him but he won't talk to you. He won't talk to anybody anymore."

"He's dead, isn't he?"

The kid gaped. "Hey, yeah! How'd you know?"

"An educated guess. How'd it happen?"

The kid made a long and indescribable Donald Duck sound as he drew his finger across his throat from ear to ear.

"When did they find him?"

"This morning. His maid came at nine-thirty and found him. She came screaming out into the lobby, you should of seen her face," he grinned. I wanted to smack him.

"Did they determine when Negri had been killed?"

"The cop says the croaker said yesterday sometime. The lab guys are up there now. Still want to go up?"

"What for?"

"Just to see."

"That's not how I get my kicks."

He started at the bruise on my forehead. "What happened to you? She cross her legs on you or something?"

"A midget hit me. You have a public phone?"

"Over there," he said, jerking his head at a booth beside a bank of elevators.

I sat down in the booth to compose my thoughts before calling Carol Quinn. There was a lot I could tell her. I could tell her that the way things looked, Al Negri, a gambler in Sam Wisniak's organization, had gotten Jimmy Quinn to shave points in last night's game and Negri had bet with both hands on the game. Only, Negri hadn't cut his boss in on the information—an act, in Wisniak's word, of disloyalty, But Negri had been too greedy and his heavy-handed wagering had scared the bookies away and caused them to suspend action on the game. Wisniak had traced the heavy bets to the source, Negri, and had had Negri's hash permanently settled.

This still didn't explain Jimmy's disappearance. What did explain Jimmy s disappearance was an alternate theory, that Al Negri had somehow double-crossed Jimmy and Jimmy had murdered Negri in retaliation. The hand that drew a knifeblade across Negri's throat might well be the same one that had completed seventeen passes for 245 yards last evening.

Nor was I clear as yet about the meaning of that list attached to Jimmy's savings passbook. Had he organized a group of bettors—ballplayers—to wager on last night's fix? Or did one thing have nothing to do with another? For that matter, could I be sure that any one element in this crazy affair had anything to do with any other?

Until I had more input, there was no sense in emotionally burdening Carol any more heavily than she was already burdened. I phoned her and assumed a speaking voice that denied the incredible events of the last few hours. "In case you haven't heard from Hobie Gilmore, we all fixed on a story this morning to explain Jimmy's absence."

"No, Hobie called me. He said we're just going to say Jimmy wrenched his shoulder and is resting it for a couple of days in seclusion."

"Right."

"They want to see me."

"See them. You know what to say. And what not to say."

"Where will you stay tonight?" she asked.

"In New York. There's some business back there I simply have to tackle and for the moment, I've come to some dead ends here. I'll wait for something to open up, then I'll come running back. The Commissioner's man is working on some leads and I expect he'll pick up the trail—he's a devilishly competent guy. Meanwhile, I want you to call me the second there's any kind of development."

"Thanks for everything," she said softly.

"Hell, I haven't done enough."

"I know." She hung up, leaving me with a tingle in my spine.

I pressed a dime into the phone and dialed a couple of digits to report to Barry Posner what I'd learned. But I changed my mind and hung up. With the information I gave him, Posner could set machinery in motion that would yank the investigation out of my hands. I wasn't prepared to deal myself out until I was convinced that that was the best thing to do.

In addition, I just didn't feel like giving that sonofabitch any help. Call it petty but let those among ye who are above pettiness cast the first stone. Fuck him, I said to myself, stepping out of the booth.

Was it my imagination, or had the sky suddenly darkened as I walked out of the building? I looked up at the heavens and said, "Sorry, Commissioner, it's nothing personal."

Chapter V

• • • •

I caught an early afternoon plane back to New York but lost an hour in the west-to-east journey so that by the time I arrived at my office on the 18th floor of the Lincoln Building on 42nd Street, across from Grand Central Terminal, it was almost seven o'clock and the place was almost deserted.

I fixed myself a drink and sorted through the activity log summarizing the day's events: important calls and meetings, synopses of important letters, receipts and payouts, etc. It was hard to believe it was only Tuesday and that I'd lost but one day away from the office. It seemed like a week. Thankfully, it had been a routine day and my two capable assistants, Dennis and Trish, had taken the baton out of my hands without losing a step. Dennis Whittie, a former American Basketball Association star, had even replaced me at the meeting with Red Auerbach without ruffling Red's feathers, making me wonder whether I was becoming dispensable.

I was about to push off for home when I noticed a pink memo sheet affixed with a rubber band to my telephone, Trish's unmistakable handiwork. Whenever she had an urgent message for me, she placed it somewhere I'd have to find it, on my typewriter platen, for instance, or hooked over a light switch. Once she taped a note to my toilet seat, knowing that sooner or later, I'd have to use it.

I unfolded her memo, a brief message penned in her loose scrawl in purple felt-tip ink. "If you dnt gt in too lte, cll me at hme, pls? Imprtnt. Trsh."

I tapped out the seven digits of Trish's apartment number on my Touch-Tone phone from memory. "Howdy. You asked me to call?" I said.

"Dave, hi! How'd it go in Indianapolis?" Her voice was still high and sweet and pleasant though it had dropped a note or two in range in the three years I'd known her, a combination of maturing and smoking.

"Uneventfully. I developed frostbite at a football game, uncorked a potentially major football scandal, got myself punched out, almost shook hands with a corpse, antagonized the Commissioner's aide, and nearly cuckolded a client. I also lost a dime in a phone booth."

I'm not sure she took me seriously. "Things were pretty dull around the office, too."

"What's up?"

"Can you come over for a drink? There's someone here I'd like you to meet."

"Male or female?"

"Male."

"I thought your memo said it was important."

"It is. He is."

"You've got a boyfriend. You're getting married."

"Dave, just come over, huh?"

I shrugged. "See you in ten minutes."

I picked up a taxi in front of the building and directed the driver to the corner of East End Avenue and 82nd Street, a staid old building in a quiet and expensive neighborhood. A far cry from the wretched East Village flat Trish had occupied three or so years ago when she'd become my secretary. But then Trish herself was a far cry from the abandoned little nymph I'd hired. She'd shed the cupcake image for the refinements of a lovely young businesswoman and with what she earned in salary and commissions working for me, she'd been able to step up to a tasteful five-room apartment and a distinctively upper-middle-class lifestyle.

She'd also become extremely valuable to me, handling with high skill a list of lucrative female athletes that seemed to expand daily. In fact, she'd been written up in such diverse publications as Ladies' Home Journal, Ms., People, Cosmopolitan, and Sports Illustrated as one of those Women-Rising-Precipitously-In-A-Man's-World. She was extremely touchy about the subject and had no sense of humor when it came to feminism as I'd discovered once when I'd teasingly called her "the head of my agency's women's auxiliary" at a sports award luncheon at the Plaza Hotel. She had pushed a plate of warm beef bourguignonne into my lap.

I'm not sure if qualms niggle but a qualm niggled me as I rode up the elevator to the eighth floor. I couldn't get it out of my head that the man Trish wanted me to meet was someone she was romantically involved with and it bothered me. She'd had countless affairs and one-night stands in the days when she was my secretary and she'd even lived with a guy for a stretch of time. All of which was cool with me because except for a few emotional ups and downs, it didn't affect her work. Even if it had, she was still, all in all, a secretary and therefore expendable (though I was so eager to keep her, I'd steadfastly refused to let her seduce me, knowing if I'd given in I'd sooner or later have had to let her go).

But now she was an executive and emotional ups and downs could easily reflect themselves in our firm's financial charts, in her handling of clients, in the way she conducted negotiations. I liked even less the prospect of her getting married if that's what she was preparing to spring on me. She'd protest how it wouldn't affect her work, how the perspective groom was very liberal or respectful of her as a person, and all that. But I could not shake the worry that I would lose her. I prayed that my anticipations were all paranoid fantasies and that the man she wanted me to meet was her interior decorator, who needed my help in determining the best color for her dining room.

But I didn't think so.

I pushed the bell and Trish greeted me with a friendly kiss on the cheek. She's a tall, slim blonde with curly ringlets, Bahama green eyes, and a saucy expression that has survived the refinement she's undergone in the last year or two. She wore a green velvet hostess pajama thing with no bra, and no slippers. On the thick lawn-green carpet she didn't need them. I stepped inside the formal foyer and into the light.

"Jesus, look at you!" She touched a cool finger to the lump on my brow. "You want some ice for that?"

"Yes. Put it in a glass with some bourbon and branch water. I'll press it to my head, then I'll drink it, and in two weeks no one will ever know I'd been knocked silly."

"What happened?"

"An elevator accident," I said. "Someone slugged me in one." I sniffed the air and inhaled the aroma of roast leg of lamb. Off the kitchen, I could see a table set for three in her spacious dining room. "Who's your other guest?" I asked, handing her my coat.

"You, if you'd like to stay. Come." She took my hand and led me into the living room, a high-ceilinged room with dark-green walls trimmed in white molding. The walls were covered with paintings, prints, and etchings of high quality. The velvet and brocade-covered chairs and sofas were, I knew from past visits, more comfortable than they looked. In fact, an extremely tall, large-boned young man was attempting to rise out of one as I entered the room. He reminded me of an army transport plane trying to lift off a short runway.

He was obviously an athlete, barrel-chested and broad-shouldered, almost popping out of his plaid slacks and white turtleneck sweater. What threw me off was the long black beard flowing out of a tangle of jet-black hair, and delicate rimless eyeglasses. Separate the head from the body and I'd have taken him for a rabbi. In fact, there was a gentility around the mouth and dark eyes, a kind of sweet humility that seemed to have been torn out of an illustrated Sunday school book about the prophets.

His handshake was gentle.

"Dave, this is Bob Rankin. Bob, Dave Bolt," said Trish, handing me my drink, probably the only good bourbon and branch water made by a non-Texan in New York City. It had taken her two years to get the formula just right.

I looked into the Abraham, Isaac, and Jacob face. "That's a name I've heard somewhere. Forgive me for not remembering where."

"He's the star running back for the Ottawa Rough Riders," Trish beamed.

"Not the star," Rankin demurred modestly. "Just a running back."

"The star," Trish insisted. There was a proprietary air in the way she looked at him that bolstered my suspicion about their relationship.

"I'm sorry, I don't follow Canadian football that closely. To me, twelve men on a football field is a five-yard penalty.

Wait a minute." I closed my eyes and fished around for something. "I think I read a piece about you in. . .?"

"Sport magazine, probably," he said.

"Right, right, right," I said, snapping my fingers. "You're the Mystery Man of the Mountains."

He winced and colored. "That was their title."

I remember it all now, not just the title but the picture that went with it, a photo of Rankin in a plaid lumberman's shirt and wool hat looking like some forest legend incarnate. Only he wasn't a forest legend but a football one, or at least one in the making. It seems that three or four years ago Rankin had simply walked into the training camp of the Ottawa Rough Riders and asked for a tryout. On his first carry, he'd dragged three defenders twelve yards and he'd pretty much been doing that ever since.

The odd thing was that nobody knew anything about him and, at the time the Sport piece came out last year, they still didn't know. He'd simply declared he grew up in the Canadian Rockies, watched a few games in Saskatchewan, decided he'd like to try it, and here he was. Some strenuous efforts by Canadian journalists to track Rankin's background down had met with minus yardage, though something like twelve sets of parents and fifteen deserted wives annually came out of the woodwork to claim him for their own. After a while, it was more fun to elaborate on the myth than try puncturing it. Rankin had been described as taciturn and hard to get to know before some idiot of a newspaper editor thought up the idea of planting a girl on him with whom he was supposed to fall in love and tell the secret of his life. Rankin found out about it and after that refused to talk to anybody about anything. "He won't even say Ouch if you break his leg," I recall one of his teammates being quoted.

"Let me guess what brings you to New York," I said making myself comfortable at one end of a sofa.

He smiled. "It shouldn't be too difficult."

"The New York Jets are what bring you to New York."

He nodded. "Yes. I'm playing out my option with Ottawa and the Jets wanted to talk to me."

"And you'd like us to handle the negotiations."

"Yes, sir."

"Seems straightforward enough," I said, wondering where the hitch was. I observed something pass between Rankin and Trish, something troubled, like an acrid blue spark that left an unpleasant after-odor. Somewhere in that spark was the hitch.

"I wish it were," Rankin said, dropping his eyes, then casting them again in Trish's direction as if waiting for her permission to speak.

"Go on, Bob. Tell him. It's okay," she said.

I leaned forward expectantly and watched him fumble with the crease of his trousers, pinching it till it was sharp enough to shave with.

"Well, you see, Rankin isn't my real name. My real name is Rubin, Robert Rubin. . . Bobby Rubin?"

The interrogative indicated I was supposed to know the name and for the second time, I found myself not quite placing it. I looked at Trish for help.

"Cornell, class of '71," Trish said.

I groped in the dark, then found the switch. "Ah, that Bobby Rubin!" Rubin had been one of the leading rushers in the country and Ivy League team or not, he'd been a very hot prospect for the pros until. . . until. . . well, just what the hell had happened to him, anyway? "Just what the hell happened to you, anyway?" I asked.

"I was drafted."

"By whom? Buffalo, wasn't it?"

"Buffalo, yes," he said sadly. "Buffalo—and the United States Army."

"I see," I said.

"No, you don't," said Trish.

"You mean you didn't do your hitch in the army, then go to Canada?"

"No."

I scratched my head a moment, then I did see. "Whoo boy. You just went to Canada."

"Yes."

"To evade the draft."

"To refuse to serve in the most immoral war of modern history," he answered. Until then his voice had been almost whisper-quiet but his declaration echoed off the walls like some Biblical commandment.

"I was just using the government's phrase," I apologized. I felt resentful apologizing, not liking to be put on the defensive. "I also believe that's the term used in the federal statute."

He turned his hands up and looked at me with quiet defiance. "Unfortunately, that's true."

The mystery of the Mystery Man of the Mountains was now easy enough to unravel. "So you disappeared into Canada and lay low, growing your beard. But you couldn't find work without the proper papers, so you offered yourself to the Rough Riders."

"That's approximately right. I do have Canadian papers, though."

"Not real ones," I said.

"I'd rather not go into that. Let's just say, if I wanted to live my life out in Canada, I could do it."

"But you don't. You want to come home."

"Yes."

"On whose terms?"

"Mine."

"Have you sounded out the government on amnesty?"

"Indirectly, through my parents."

"And?"

"Well, as you probably know, Mr. Ford's clemency program expired back in the spring of 1975—along with the war. At long last. . ."

"Why didn't you negotiate while the clemency program was still in effect?"

"I did but their position was unacceptable. Among other things, they wanted me to sign a statement whose wording was a complete negation of everything I believe in, everything I left the country for. . ."

Trish took my glass away and refilled it while I sat, elbows on knees, contemplating this kid's bind. It was a cruel one, all right, and no less pitiable because it was completely of his own making. Yet I did feel less concern than I should have and I wondered why. Although I'd originally greeted our involvement in Vietnam with about forty percent as much enthusiasm as every other patriotic Southern white man, by the late 1960s, I'd certainly run out of excuses like everybody else and the war was as big an embarrassment to me as it was to our nation's leaders. In other words, intellectually I agreed with Rubin. And yet his arrogant doctrinairism turned me off.

Why, hell, that was it—it was his goddamned arrogance! Beneath that humble, long-suffering exterior beat the heart of a crusader. I just don't think I liked Bob Rubin is what it was.

"Can you help him, Dave?" Trish asked, slipping my drink back into my hand and refilling Rubin's drained wineglass with a fresh dollop of sherry.

"How?" I asked her. We talked to each other as if he weren't in the room.

"I don't know; I thought you might speak to the Commissioner."

"What can he do? This is between Bob and the government. I mean, sure, if Bob were just a garden-variety football player wanting to move from Canada to here, no sweat! I could hammer down a contract for him in two minutes. But he's not. He didn't want to sign the government's statement and he didn't want to take the job Uncle Sam offered him. Now he wants to come back but now there's no more goddamn machinery for dealing with him. Technically, he's a fugitive from justice. Until he makes his peace with the government, no one can do a thing for him—not me, not the Jets, not the Commissioner himself. And there's something else to think about, too."

Trish covered Bob's hand, openly confirming the status of their relationship, and they listened to me with stunned eyes.

"Even if Bob got his way, even if he was able to simply walk back into the country and get himself pardoned one hundred percent—not much of a likelihood, even with our President's track record in the pardoning department—Bob's presence on an American football team could be controversial and possibly divisive. Bob could be unpopular with the fans, he might even be unpopular with his teammates. There are still people who somehow feel they must justify the war. I just don't know how everyone's going to take it when they find out who 'Bob Rankin' is. And I'm certainly not going to be party to representing you under any other name but your real one."

"I'm not asking you to," the kid said, squeezing his wineglass dangerously hard. "I'm just asking you to help me figure out what to do."

"What to do is stop trying to have it both ways, my friend. You made a decision. The government made a decision about your decision and they're not going to back down. That puts the game squarely back in your own territory and on your own two-yard line, at that. As I see it, you have only three choices. Go back to Canada and be the Mystery Man. Your secret's safe with us, believe me. Or you can come into the country, reveal your identity, accept the government's terms, and hope for mercy. In which case, I'll help you every way I can. Or you can come into the country, reveal your identity, stick to your guns, and fight it out. In which case I'll write to you regularly in Leavenworth. But you can't—I repeat, can't—have it all your way."

"Why not? The government had it both ways. They had their war across the sea and their peace here, their destruction there and their war economy prosperity here, their. . ."

He had me there. I looked at Trish and said, "I never did fare well in these deep intellectual discussions."

But Trish was far from sympathetic to me. "It's not intellectual, Dave. Bob is living proof that the Vietnam War is still wounding people and ruining their lives. The fighting's over, at last, but the issues are still with us."

Bob squeezed her hand and looked at me patronizingly. "Forget it, Trish. He doesn't understand."

That rankled me considerably. "Hey now, my friend, I may look dumb. . ."

"I didn't say you were dumb," he replied, trying to sound respectful. But it came out arrogant.

I felt extremely uncomfortable. Tempting though the aroma of roast leg of lamb was, I would have been miserable staying for dinner. I got to my feet, shaking my head. "I don't know what else to say, son. I just don't think we can do anything for you."

"We?" said Trish, cocking her eyebrows.

The arch significance of her question flew completely past me as I quickly replied, "Yes, we." I looked back at Rubin. "Perhaps there are other agents who will back up your 'Bob Rankin' charade. I'll be glad to give you the names of my colleagues and you can try them yourself. But include us out." I looked at Trish and said, "Sorry, I can't stay for dinner. I have a previous engagement."

She knew it was a lie but made no effort to press me to stay. She looked as uncomfortable as I felt, except that it was I, not Rubin, who was making her uncomfortable. "Sure, Dave. I'll see you tomorrow."

Grudgingly, I shook Rubin's hand and retreated out of the apartment.

The cool air was refreshing and the walk to my apartment on 77th Street gave me a chance to review my behavior. I decided I was not particularly proud of it and in fact I felt a little foolish. I knew I'd let my personal dislike of Rubin cloud my thinking processes. There probably was something I could do for him if I were motivated to. I just wasn't motivated to, that's all. But it wasn't until the following morning that I understood why I wasn't and by then it was almost too late.

Chapter VI

• • • •

I passed a poorish night, hounded by turbulent dreams in which I was stalked in turn by Sam Wisniak and Midget, Barry Posner, the Mystery Man of the Mountains, the doorman at Al Negri's building, Carol Quinn's kids, the Commissioner—even Red Auerbach got in the picture. I dragged my ass out of bed at six-thirty, showered, and tanked up on coffee while going through the newspapers.

Both the New York Times and the Daily News carried the story we'd concocted about Jimmy Quinn recovering from a sore shoulder in some warm-weather hideaway. The stories were only a couple of lines long and buried among the miscellaneous chitchat columns about sports people in the news. That was good—neither paper had assigned any particular significance to the item.

A little after eight, I left for work, strolling to the corner of 77th Street and Lexington Avenue, picking up the Lexington Avenue subway to Grand Central, and crossing 42nd Street to my building. Gillian, the receptionist, hadn't arrived yet, nor had Dennis Whittie. But Trish's door was closed and her typewriter was clacking away. I thought of looking in on her then decided against it. She was undoubtedly sore at me and if I left her alone, she'd come around in her own good time.

I hung up my coat, unbuttoned my collar and pulled my tie-knot loose, and sat down at my desk. On it was a letter typed under the letterhead of my firm, Red Dog Players Management Agency. It was addressed to me. My eyes darted to the bottom of the page. The signature was Trish's. I read the text.

Dear Dave:

With this letter, I am tendering my resignation from the firm. I believe two weeks should be sufficient time for you to find a replacement.

I would appreciate an opportunity to discuss with you the terms of my departure at your earliest convenience.

I put the letter down and stared at it, dumbfounded. I reached for the phone to buzz Trish but my hand was shaking with a combination of rage and a kind of fear. I was in no fit condition to speak to her yet. I got up, paced the room, and finally broke my rule of no drinking before one P.M. I broke it by more than four hours, but the bourbon spread a soothing glow over my body and I sat down at my desk again, fairly calm. I picked up the phone and dialed 2. I heard the raucous buzz of Trish's phone through the adjoining wall.

She picked up and I said, "Shall we talk?"

Her voice was clogged as if she'd been crying. "I'll be right in."

A moment later she was standing before me, dressed in the demure tweed skirt and ruffled blouse she'd traded for the outrageously sexy garments she'd worn when she first came to work for me. I looked at her, absorbing, perhaps for the first time, the full impact of her growth into handsome womanhood. Her eyes were slightly glassy, betraying a degree of remorse that was chillingly absent from her resignation letter.

I gestured to the guest chair in front of my desk and she lowered herself into it tensely.

"I'm not going to contest your decision," I said. "I just think I'm owed an explanation."

She shrugged, trying to appear insouciant. But the tremor in her voice gave her away. "I've. . . decided to go out on my own."

"Set up your own agency, you mean?"

"Yes."

"What're you going to do for clients?"

She stiffened slightly. "Some of my present clients will come with me."

I'd anticipated that reply. "Not if they don't want to face a breach-of-contract suit. You know what our contract reads. They're bound to this agency—my agency—not to you."

She'd anticipated my reply, too. "I don't think you'd hold them against their will."

"You'd better be certain of that before you invite any of them to come away with you," I said sternly, meaning it.

She looked at me squarely and knew I wasn't bluffing. Then she shrugged again. "Then I'll start from scratch."

"Who with? Bob Rubin?" I tried to keep the irony out of my voice but wasn't very successful.

Her eyes flashed. "Yes, Bob Rubin."

I lowered my voice. "Trish, isn't he what this is really all about?"

"No, not really. He's just the. . . the catalyst for a lot of other dissatisfactions."

I raised my eyebrows. "Come on, sweetheart. You don't have any other serious dissatisfactions working with me and you know it. You're well compensated, I leave you alone, I respect you, I. . . I even. . ." I gulped back something. "I can't believe you have any major complaints. It comes back to last night, admit it."

"You treated him disgracefully, yes, I'll admit that."

"I treated him objectively and if you weren't so personally involved with him—I mean, you have been sleeping with him, haven't you?—you'd see it easily. Trish, this. . . this tantrum is all on account of the fact that you've lost your head over the guy."

"And what about your tantrum?" she snapped back angrily.

"My tantrum? I don't recall any—"

"You don't call that blatant display of hostility last night a tantrum? Talk about being personally involved!"

"You can scarcely accuse me of being personally involved with Bob Rubin!" I laughed.

"Who said anything about your being involved with Bob Rubin?" she came back, gaping at me as if I were insane.

"Then who. . .?"

"Me, asshole! Me!"

"You? I'm personally involved with you?" I laughed, wondering if I wasn't indeed a trifle barmy.

"You really can't see it, can you?"

"See what, Trish? See what?"

"How jealous you are!"

I was on the verge of babbling deliriously. "Jealous of. . .?"

"Of Bob. Jealous of his taking me away from you."

I misunderstood her entirely. "How can he take something away from me that doesn't belong to me? Considering that we've never slept together, I hardly have any claim on you."

"But you have a claim on me, whether we've slept together or not."

"I. . ." Suddenly the shaft penetrated and a hot blush of shame flooded my cheeks. "If you mean that I need you. . ." I looked at her, wondering if I could entrust her with the admission. Or would she take it for weakness and trample on it?

She read my mind. "You can say it, Dave. I won't hurt you. I'd. . . I'd like to hear you say it." Her angry face had softened and her eyes glistened with incipient tears.

I pushed away from my desk, came around to her, took her hands and raised her to her feet. She slipped into my arms and I held her tightly. "Haven't I told you how much I need you?" I murmured into her ear, inhaling the sweet fragrance that wafted up from her neck.

"Not lately. Not enough."

I kissed her, not passionately, yet in a way that transcended passion, if that doesn't sound overly sentimental. "You've become a part of me, like a limb. If I've taken you for granted, I'm sorrier than I can say."

She pushed away, wiping the tears off her cheeks with the back of her hand. Then she leaned over the desk and picked up her resignation letter. She started to tear it in half but I stopped her and took it away from her. "No, I think I'd like to keep it. In fact, I think I'll have it framed so I can look at it whenever I get too confident. And as for Bob Rubin—well, maybe there is something I can do. I'd like to think about it. I've got one thought."

She squeezed my hand. "Thanks, Dave." Now she squirmed a little with embarrassment. "Well, got to get back to my desk."

She pivoted gracefully and started for the door. "Hey, Trish?" I called after her.

She turned. "Huh?"

"You've come a long way, baby."

"Thanks, Dave."

That catastrophe averted, I tackled the day's round of chores, working swiftly and hard, pursued by an inkling that the next event in the Jimmy Quinn affair would momentarily obtrude and I'd be off and running. A little after eleven, the prophecy was fulfilled. It came in the form of a phone call from Carol Quinn.

"You got home safely," she said.

"Yes, thanks."

"Something odd has happened. I thought you'd like to know."

"Shoot."

"I've gotten four or five phone calls this morning. From football players wanting to know if the story about Jimmy is true."

"What's odd about that?"

"They're not Racers—except one, Saul Talcott. And their initials. . ."

"Match those on the list? Hot damn, new we're getting somewhere. Who were they?"

"The first was Ricky Lindner of the Forty-niners."

"Go on," I said, jotting the name down and underlining first initials.

"Carl Janeway of the Chicago Bears, Buddy Esterbrook of the St. Louis Cardinals, Shorty LeBrun of New England, and Ladrue Retting of the Jets."

I reached into my pocket and removed the list from Jimmy's passbook. I put check marks next to S. T., R. L., C. J., B. E., S. L., and L. R. "Tell me, did Jimmy know these guys? I mean, other than professionally?"

"Yes. I mean, some better than others. For instance, Jimmy and Ricky Lindner were fraternity brothers, and Shorty LeBrun went to school with Jimmy, but they weren't in the same fraternity. Buddy Esterbrook is an engineer, and

I think they became friends at a convention. Carl Janeway
is married to a girl Jimmy used to date, and Ladrue Retting
is a Players' Representative, same as Jimmy."

"So, it's like a loose confederation of friends."

"I guess. But beyond that, I still don't know what it all
means."

"I don't, either, but I think—hold on." I put Carol on
hold and buzzed Dennis Whittie. "Dennis, are the Jets
playing at home this week?"

"Uh-huh. Denver."

"Thanks." I punched Carol back on and said. "The Jets
are in town. I think I'll have a chat with Ladrue Retting.
He's a client of mine. Tell me, how did these guys sound
when they called?"

"Oh, casual, but concerned, if you know what I mean."

"Did you ask them why they were calling?"

"Yes, but they all just said, 'Oh, just want to know if
Jimmy's all right'."

"I see. Well, stand by for more NFL action. I'll call you
after I've spoken to Ladrue. Give the kids a kiss."

I drove out to the Hofstra College campus on Long Island where the Jets were just breaking for lunch after their
morning workout. Ladrue Retting, a leggy special-team
man with a freckled, light-brown face, shiny straight black
hair and a droopy walrus mustache, was perspiring pro-
fusely despite the below-freezing weather when I collared
him as he clack-clacked up the wooden ramp to the locker
room. Perhaps I was reading into his face but it seemed
preoccupied with something other than football.

"Ladrue?"

He looked up and stared before recognition swept his
face on the wings of a bright smile. "Hey, Dave, how's it
goin'?" he said, giving me The Grip. "Sorry I didn't recog-

nize you for a second there. Just didn't expect to see you."

"I was wondering if I can nab you for a chat before you sit down to eat."

"I'll check with Coach. What's up?"

"Just check with Coach."

His open grin narrowed to taut anxiety and he eyed me suspiciously. He disappeared into the locker room, and I waited for ten minutes just inside the door, beneath the humorless gaze of a private policeman. At length, Ladrue trucked out smartly, dressed in tan slacks, a thick turtleneck sweater, and high-heeled shoes. His hair glistened with dampness. "Coach made me shower first," he apologized.

"Can we go somewhere private?"

"Mm—there's a student lounge next to the cafeteria upstairs."

"Fine."

We marched up a flight of stairs and past the cafeteria where the Jets were filing in for lunch. Rich Caster and Emerson Boozer recognized me and saluted me. Assistant Defensive Coach Al Rittlinger gave me the evil eye, wondering what an agent was doing hanging around his team.

We entered a large, quiet room decorated in blue. It was vacant but I picked the corner farthest from the door and kept looking over my shoulder as I talked.

"Now, what's it all about, Dave?" he asked, taking a pack of Kools out of his pocket, lighting one, and waving the smoke away. It was a fine if his coach caught him.

I came on strong. "Why did you call Carol Quinn this morning?"

He tried to suppress his surprise but his brows arched involuntarily. He recovered and said, "Jimmy's a friend of mine. Just wanted to wish him well."

"A lot of football players called today to wish him well."

My client squirmed out of the closing trap. "He's a popular guy."

"It's an interesting thing, Ladrue. Jimmy kept a list in a strongbox, a list of initials. Beside each pair of initials was a sum of money. And what's interesting is, everyone who called Carol Quinn this morning matched those initials."

"That a fact?" said Ladrue, forehead dampening though the room was cold. He dragged deep on his cigarette.

"Jimmy had you down for $7500, Ladrue. I want to know what it's all about."

"Dave," he said, putting his hand on my knee. "We're friends, right?"

"Yes."

"Then do me a favor? Don't ask."

"I have to, Ladrue. Jimmy's disappeared."

"Uh-oh. I was afraid of that." He swallowed loudly.

"That's why you called Carol, isn't it? To find out if Jimmy had. . ." I thought it through for a moment. "To find out if Jimmy had absconded with your money?"

"Yes." He smashed the stub of his cigarette out and lit another. "Coach would have my ass totaled if he saw me smokin' this way."

"Ladrue, right now I'm the only person who knows about Jimmy's list—me and Carol. But the Commissioner's office has a man on the case. The longer it goes, the more the pressure's going to build up, because if Jimmy doesn't show up for next Sunday's game, the shit's gonna hit the fan. I may have to turn this list over to the Commissioner. If that happens, you're really gonna see some asses totaled. Now, I don't know what this list means but I can think of some very evil interpretations. Are you sure you wouldn't like to clue me in?"

He took a deep inhale and a gusty exhale. "Okay. Do

you remember last winter, after the season was over, I came to you asking for your advice about how to invest my savings?"

"Yes."

"Remember I told you how Smiley Kruger had made some fast bucks for me and some other guys?"

The light began to filter into my benighted brain. "Yes, yes I do." Smiley Kruger was a former Baltimore Colts offensive lineman, retired some five or six years. He'd gone into investment counseling, specializing in the management of ballplayers' money. His vast contacts, built up over fourteen years in the NFL, gave him a ready-made field in which to sow his seeds.

But the thing about Smiley Kruger was, a lot of his investment schemes were dubious. He'd gotten into trouble for selling hamburger chain franchises he didn't own and was sued for fraud by Jackie Sneider of the Los Angeles Rams. I think the case was settled out of court.

Unfortunately, there was always a new crop of suckers to buy Kruger's line of jive. Ladrue had been one of them. He'd lured Ladrue into his spiderweb by taking a thousand dollars from him and converting it into two thousand the following week on what Kruger claimed was some legitimate hedge deal in the stock market.

Kruger had then asked Ladrue if he wanted to spring for a little heavier action. Fortunately, that's when Ladrue and I were sitting down to work out a sensible investment plan. Ladrue had told me about Kruger's scheme and I'd said, Definitely Not.

Ladrue now looked at me, then hung his head. "Well, I didn't listen to your advice."

"You mean, you gave Kruger more money in spite of my warning?"

"Not Kruger, no. I mean, not directly. I gave it to Jimmy."

"Why Jimmy?"

"Well, Jimmy was kind of organizing things for Kruger. He was like the collector, if you see what I mean."

"Kruger's front," I said, putting a sharper point on it. "Kruger's shill," I said, honing it finer still.

"What do you mean?"

"Don't you see? Kruger probably ran into resistance when he started hitting you guys up for big bread. He needed someone to do it for him, someone with a reputation for sincerity and impeccable honesty. So he got Jimmy." I handed Jimmy's passbook to Ladrue. "Check this."

Ladrue studied it and looked up. "Yeah, that's about right."

"What do you mean?"

"Well, when Jimmy approached me, he told me he had this friend who'd parlayed Jimmy's small investment into a big return. This passbook confirms it."

"Did Jimmy tell you who the friend was?"

"He was reluctant to but he finally admitted it was Kruger. So I said, 'Jimmy, I've been touted off doing business with Smiley Kruger.' But Jimmy said. 'Hell, Ladrue, your money is safer with him than it is in a bank. I don't know how he does it but he's got Lady Luck locked!' So I gave Jimmy twenty-five hundred bucks and a month later it came back seventy-five hundred."

"I'm sure it did. So now Jimmy hit you up for seventy-five hundred."

"Yes. He hit a number of his friends up. We jokingly called ourselves the Special Team but now I'm thinking we should have named it the Suicide Squad."

"What was the money for?"

"An Australian land deal. Kruger told Jimmy he had an option on a parcel of undeveloped oceanfront land in western

Australia at four dollars an acre. Kruger said he'd lined up some big syndicate to develop the land for a resort, maybe make us ten, twenty times our kick-in, or more." He looked at me pointedly. "You think Kruger was setting us up?"

"I don't know."

"You think Jimmy was setting us up?"

"I don't know that, either. I just know Jimmy's disappeared."

"Disappeared with my money."

"Disappeared with a lot of people's money."

He pounded his knee and reached for another cigarette. I took it out of his hand.

"That's not going to get your money back."

He snatched the cigarette back, lit it with shaking hands, and looked at me bleakly. "Ain't nothin' gonna get my money back. All I own is the smoke in my lungs. Don't take that away from me, too, huh?"

Chapter VII

••••

I'd been tempted to sound Ladrue out about a possible connection between Jimmy's involvement in the Kruger investment syndicate and Al Negri's wager on the Monday night game. But I didn't think Ladrue would even be aware of the latter. Furthermore, I didn't want him to know about it—it would travel across the grapevine faster than a laser beam and by tomorrow morning would be a headline on the sports page. What I didn't know, as I got back into my car and pushed off for Manhattan, was that it already was a headline on the sports page—the sports page of New York's afternoon newspaper, the Post, and over the byline of my closest friend, Roy Lescade.

I saw it when I garaged my car on 41st Street off Lexington Avenue. The early edition lay on the table in the attendant's booth, front page down. In bold black letters across the top of the back page blared the headline,

Qb's "Injury" And Gambler's Death—Linked?

"Mind if I read this?" I said to the attendant, a rotund Puerto Rican.

"Help yourself," he shrugged.

I helped myself to a frighteningly accurate article speculating on the relationship between the shutdown of gambling on the Racer-Lion game, Al Negri's murder, and Jimmy Quinn's so-called injury and sudden inaccessibility. I don't know where Roy had gotten his information, whether someone had called him anonymously, or the Commissioner's office had intentionally leaked it, or whether Roy had simply put two and two together from information available to every other reporter. Whatever the answer, the black print turned rage-red in my eyes and my hands shook so violently with anger you could hear the paper rattling over the revving of car engines and the shriek of tires in the garage.

I took my ticket stub from the attendant and stepped out of the garage and into a cab. "Two-ten South Street," I barked.

I brooded over Roy Lescade's betrayal as the taxi blended into southbound traffic on Lexington Avenue, headed for the New York Post's offices. Roy and I had started out on opposite sides of football's gladiatorial pit, I a tight end on the Texas University Longhorns, he a linebacker for one of our traditional rivals, Texas A&M. Every year of our varsity days would find him and me popping each other into oblivion and in the summer after graduation, he invited me to spend a month on his ranch in Brownsville, Texas, on the Mexican border. We became fast friends. Then I spurned a number of bids from professional teams in order to join the army while Roy was drafted by the Chicago Bears. He was cut from the team—just didn't want it enough. I got out of the service and signed up with the Dallas Cowboys.

Roy got into journalism, for which he'd always shown considerable talent, and in due time was writing for a Dallas newspaper. It was Roy, half out of friendship and half out of newspaperman's instinct for a human-interest story, who decided to track down the drunken stumblebum Dave Bolt, found him, brought him around, and got him his job in the Cowboy front office. I owed Roy my life.

And I had repaid him, giving him many an inside story over the years. Of course, not too long ago I'd promised him a very big story, the story behind the beating up of a baseball player client of mine, Willie Hesketh, who had dared to cross the picket line during the pre-season players' strike. Then I'd had second thoughts about the wisdom of publishing the story and withheld it from Roy. It had pissed him off considerably and he'd been frigidly formal with me since the spring. But I couldn't believe he'd publish the Jimmy Quinn story without at least checking with me first.

I barged up to the security desk in the lobby of the Post building and had the guard call up to Roy's office. A moment later, he waved me through, droning, "Third floor."

I stepped out of the elevator on the third floor and turned right, threading my way through a catacomb of partitions and cubicles until I came to a bank of formal offices lined up on either side of a carpeted corridor. Here the metallic clatter of typewriters was subdued and the stale smell of ancient cigarette smoke not so noticeable. Roy, who reminds me of a life-size teddy bear with the stuffing redistributed, was leaning out of his door waiting for me, his hair hanging over his brow like a bison's scruffy shag, his cheeks stubbly with unshaved prickles. His loose slacks, white-on-white shirt, and stained thin tie looked like a rag-picker's rejects, all rumpled and smeared with black streaks where he apparently wiped his hands after fiddling with his typewriter ribbon.

As I approached, he sounded me out with a friendly smile. Getting a distinctly unfriendly response as I glowered at him, he backed into his office and balled his fist as if preparing for an assault. I wasn't sure but that he had reason; I was mad enough to take a swing at him. But I stopped in his doorway and glared. "How could you print that, you big fuck?"

He held up his hands and backed behind his desk. "Hey now, hey now."

"Answer my question."

"I got a press card, is how."

"I'm in no mood for smart-ass remarks. Where'd you get the information?"

"Wire services and a few phone calls?" Roy spoke in question marks.

"Why didn't you call me before you ran the story?"

"I did. You was out, buddy. Ask your receptionist, that English flip-flop? You'll find a message."

"You couldn't wait till I called you back?"

"I had a deadline, pal."

"You couldn't let it go till tomorrow?"

"Sure, and let Dick Young and Red Smith scoop me? Assuming they're as smart as me, of course."

"So this is all your theory, in other words."

"Not entirely theory, pardner. There's some rather compelling evidence?"

"Circumstantial."

"No law against using circumstantial evidence? Hell, there'd be no sports page if we waited for truth."

I shook my head disgustedly. "I never thought I'd hear you talk that way."

"Whyn't you sit down and calm down and let me make you a drink?"

"I only drink with friends," I snapped.

"No wonder you stay so sober," he retorted.

I paced the room for a moment, letting some adrenaline drain away. "I can't help feeling you did this to spite me."

He fluttered his eyes innocently. "Why, what would I do that for, aside from the fact that you screwed me out of the Willie Hesketh story last spring?"

"I told you I'd make that up to you."

"How long was I supposed to wait? Besides, if I had to consult with you and ask your permission every time I had a story about one of your clients, I'd be in pretty sad shape, now, wouldn't I?"

He held back a grin but I could see from the delight in his eyes that he was savoring his revenge. "Roy, you've unleashed more damage than the Galveston hurricane with your irresponsible story."

"Irresponsible? Only if it has no basis in fact. And speaking of fact, maybe you could fill in some gaps for me?"

"Roy, I wouldn't tell you it was dark out at midnight. And as for having a basis in fact, when Jimmy Quinn hits you with a libel suit, you'll find your basis in fact."

I'm sure Roy had heard threats like that more often than he could count. He simply turned his palms up and said, "All Jimmy has to do is stick his face out of 'seclusion' long enough to deny my story."

"I'll remember this, bastard," I grunted.

"You do that, my friend. And while you're remembering, remember this, too: the next time you have a good story, you share it with your old buddy Roy Lescade. I trust you can find your way out of here?"

I had only the time it took to get from the Post offices to the Lincoln Building to brood about the evanescence of friendship, for when I walked into my office there was a veritable shish kabob of phone messages impaled on the chrome needle on my desk where memos were supposed to be brought to my attention. As I could have anticipated, the top one was from the Commissioner.

The second was from Carol Quinn and the rest were from representatives of the media. I summoned Trish and Dennis and we framed the wording of a press release denying Roy's story and denouncing his irresponsibility.

Dennis tapped the Commissioner's message with a long, bony finger. "And what about this one?"

"I'll tell you in a second," I said, gazing at it as if it had been written in fire. I reached for the phone and called Carol Quinn.

"Dave, thank God. Have you been trying to get through to me?" She sounded hoarse and tired. "The phone's been ringing for two hours straight."

"I'll bet it has. What have you been telling people?"

"That I'm shocked, appalled, the story is a tissue of disgraceful lies. . . But Dave, you never told me about Al Negri's murder." She was a trifle irritated.

"I didn't see the need to, since there was no verifiable link between it and Jimmy's disappearance."

"This Roy Lescade found a link."

"This Roy Lescade will pay for it, don't worry. Now look, you've got to hold the line on all this questioning by reporters. In fact, maybe you'd like to remove yourself and the kids someplace for a while."

"I thought of that. Dave, have you been able to learn anything more?"

"As a matter of fact, I have. Does the name Smiley Kruger mean anything to you?"

"Why, yes. He's a friend of Jimmy's."

"Exactly how did Jimmy describe the friendship?"

"Oh, Kruger would come into town from time to time and they'd go drinking together. I believe they had some kind of business together but Jimmy never said much about it." I could hear her snap her fingers. "Oh, how dumb of me! You think Kruger may be involved. . . I should have thought of him."

"Do me a favor. Look in your address book, the one next to your phone? See if Jimmy has a number written down for Smiley Kruger."

The phone clunked as she set it down, and I could hear her shuffling through the leaves of the address book. After a moment she came back on. "No, there's nothing here under K. Except. . ."

"Except what?"

"Well, there's a number written down here, faintly in pencil. But there's no name or address. Just a number: 861-9384."

"No area code?"

"No. Eight-six-one is a local exchange."

"Uh-huh." I thought about it for a second, wondering if it were worth a flight out to Indianapolis. I might well discover the number belonged to Jimmy's shirt maker or insurance broker, or maybe a girlfriend who had nothing to do with the case.

"I can just call it and see who answers," Carol said.

"No, because if it's Kruger, we might scare him away."

"What should we do?"

I sighed. "I'm coming out there." I turned to Trish and asked her to call TWA and let me know the next flight out. Carol held on till Trish returned. "I'll be on Flight 616 out of LaGuardia, arriving 5:30 your time."

"I'll meet you."

"Great."

"Dave?"

"Yes."

"I really need you."

"Hang tough till 5:30," I said, hanging up.

Dennis still had his finger on the Commissioner's message. "Okay, what about this?"

"Call him and tell him I'm out of town, you don't know where."

Dennis's eyes bulged and he gulped. "Uh-uh, I ain't about to hang no bell on that cat's neck! He's got enough juice to blast us to kingdom come."

I looked sharply at him. "Is this the same Dennis Whittie who could drive through a tunnel of Kentucky Colonels' arms to sink a lay-up?" Dennis had been an American Basketball Association star before an injury knocked him out of commission.

He shook his head. "Dave, all that took was physical courage. Facing the Commissioner with a lie calls for moral courage, in which I'm notably deficient."

"You'll be notably deficient in a job if you don't do it, Dennis. Look, I've got an inside track on the figure behind this mess. If I can just buy a little time to locate him. . ." I smiled. "Christmas is coming, Dennis. It's a time when employers bestow openhanded munificence on loyal employees—if they've a mind to. If those employees have demonstrated a dedication, a devotion. . ."

"You really think I would stick my head on the Commissioner's chopping block for money?" Dennis huffed righteously.

"I'll do it," Trish volunteered.

"Now hold on, hold on!" Dennis snapped. "I didn't say I wouldn't do it. . ."

"That's my man," I said, patting his hand.

Chapter VIII

• • • •

The cloud cover over Indianapolis was so thick and low, the airport lights didn't reveal themselves until a bare minute before the 707's wheels touched down on the rain-glossed runway. Heavy rivulets of water streaked horizontally across the plane's portholes, then vertically as the jet-brakes roared and slowed us to taxiing speed.

I shuffled out of the cabin, picking up my overnighter from the pretty brunette stewardess who'd paid me an enticing amount of attention during the flight and strode through the covered platform and into the terminal. I spied Carol in the crowd around the security barrier, wearing a handsome fur-lined raincoat with a hood and clutching the collars of her children to prevent them from running amuck. She planted a kiss on my cheek and carried my overnighter while I carried Teddy and Emily in each arm. Teddy informed me that Emily had swallowed a gumball without chewing it. Emily said that Teddy had stuck her toothbrush in poopoo in the toilet.

I lectured the kids on the questionable ethics of ratting on one's brother or sister while Carol brought the car around from the mazelike bowels of the garage. Rain pummeled the roof and hood of the station wagon as we steered cautiously into traffic. It took about twenty minutes to reach home.

As we wound through Beechwood's tortuous suburban streets, I looked at my watch. "Almost six. I guess the business office at the phone company is closed by now."

"I'm sure of it," Carol said. "Why?"

"I want to see if I can get a line on an address for that phone number."

"I might be able to help you there. I know a supervisor down there. I don't know if she's still there, but we can try her first thing tomorrow morning."

"Good. Have you found a place to stay?"

"A couple of friends have offered to put us up, but I really don't want to impose—they have small houses and their own kids. I booked a motel reservation. There's one a few miles from here. I just want to pack some things, then we. . ."

"We?"

She pursed her lips, "Well, you've got to stay somewhere tonight, too."

"True."

"Your room adjoins mine. You can lock your door or not, according to your scruples."

"What about your scruples?" I said.

"My door will be unlocked," she said.

"What's scruples?" Teddy inquired.

Carol laughed. "They're a brand of breakfast cereal."

"Scruples are reservations," I told Teddy. "We have reservations at a motel."

"Uncle Dave has more reservations than I do," Carol said as we turned into Alvin Court.

We slogged through the downpour up the slate path to the front door. Carol inserted the key and we stepped inside, letting the water drain off on a shag rug in the hall. Carol tilted her head. "That's funny."

"What's funny?"

"It's ice-cold in here. I had the heat up and the windows closed when I left the house. . ." She stepped into the living room. "Dave."

I followed her in. She clutched my arm with one hand and pointed with the other to the door that opened to the backyard. The storm glass was shattered and the door itself ajar. Someone had broken into the house. I pulled Carol quickly into the hall. "Whoever it was may still be here. Get into the car with the kids, start your engine, and back into the street. Be prepared to move out fast if I don't come out in a minute or two. What's the name of the motel?"

"It's the Holiday Inn in Brooktown."

"Go there. I'll call or come. If you don't hear from me within a half-hour, call the police. Scat!"

She gathered up the children and fled down the path. A moment later I heard her car start.

I stood stock-still in the hallway, listening. I heard nothing but the drubbing of rain on the roof and the pounding of my heart in my chest cavity. After a minute, I edged along the carpeted hallway toward the master bedroom. I didn't know who had broken in but I suspected what it was they'd broken in for and it was in the bedroom. I poked my head into the kids' room. It was dark but empty. I slid beyond it to the master bedroom door. It was half open and the room was damnably dark. Through the door, I could make out the dresser, part of the bed, and the closet door. The closet door was open and. . . I squinted. There was a metallic object on the floor in front of it, and papers scattered around it on the rug. The strongbox.

If the intruder was still here, he'd be behind the door,

out of my line of vision. I stood indecisively a moment then made up my mind. I hurled myself against the door.

It struck something both soft and hard, a man's belly and head respectively, and I heard a grunt and the splintering sound of the door splitting. I whipped into the room, grabbing behind the door with my left hand and connecting with the sleeve of a sweater. Beneath the sleeve was an arm that was either encased in armor or composed of muscle harder than stone. I yanked and the rest of the man came with it, an immense lump of a man whose free left fist impacted on my ribs like a piece of granite. But I had a clear shot at his face with my right and I found his jaw with it, evoking the satisfying double sound of my knuckles on his bone and his upper and lower teeth snapping together. "Motherfucker!" he bellowed in a baritone whose inflection was distinctively black.

He came on like a pulling guard in an end sweep, bulling me with his chest and steel-muscled-belly to the bed. I fell back on it and kicked out at his groin, but caught only his stomach, with absolutely no effect. I pushed off and rolled off the other side of the bed, trying to scamper to my feet. But he lunged across the bed and cuffed me, not with his right fist but with his right forearm, the forearm I'd felt some kind of armor on. I now was able to verify that it was definitely armor, by virtue of the hollow thump it made on my skull as he scored a direct hit. A multimedia show of lights and sounds exploded in my head and I heard myself cursing and moaning in some netherworld of semi-consciousness. I covered my head for a second blow but it never came. Dimly, I heard him shuffling out of the room, motherfuckering all the way. I tried to climb to my feet but my legs seemed to be made out of Jell-O before it's had a chance to set. I closed my eyes, pondering the significance of that right forearm, something in my brain telling me it was important. But my poor brain had enough to do exhorting the rest of my system to remain calm and await further instructions.

The further instructions were apparently something like, "Fuck it," because I passed out.

I awoke to the soothing warmth of a damp washcloth swabbing away the blood that had trickled down my temple and over my cheek. I opened my eyes to find Carol kneeling over me, smiling through tears. Over her shoulder, two cherubic faces gazed with clinical interest at the operation. "See?" said Teddy. "I told you he wasn't dead."

I closed my eyes again, muttering, "No, she was right, Teddy. I am dead. I am definitely dead." My skull throbbed as if it encaged a living creature pounding to get out.

"See?" said Emily. "He is dead." She started to cry.

I opened my eyes again and pushed up on my elbows. "I was only kidding, honey." I reached past Carol and touched the little girl's hand. She snuffled a few times, then, seemingly satisfied, asked her brother if he wanted to play knock-hockey.

They toddled off to their room.

"I saw him," Carol said, putting a pillow under my head. "He was a big black man. He ran out the front door and out of the lane. He had a car parked down the street. I didn't see it. Oh, Dave. . ." She started to cry and cradled my head against her breasts, a form of therapy I enthusiastically recommend.

I got to my feet shakily and sat down on the edge of the bed, letting the throbs in my skull subside while Carol fetched aspirin and coffee. She sat beside me watching concernedly as I imbibed the hot brew. "He was after that list, I'm sure of it," I said.

"Who? Who do you think it was?"

"Honey, my brainpan still has scrambled eggs in it. I can't think yet. Have you packed?"

"No."

"Do it and let's get out of here. I think I'll close my eyes a minute or two till you're ready."

I must have dozed because the next thing I knew Carol was in her coat rocking my shoulder with her hand. There was a new pain I hadn't been aware of before, in my shoulder and ribs where the goliath had first smitten me. But the catnap had been to good effect, not just in restoring me but in bringing me closer to the identity of the intruder, at least in negative terms. I knew who it wasn't. It wasn't Midge, Sam Wisniak's bodyguard. In my tortured sleep, I had dreamed about him, dreamed about our fight in the elevator, and I remembered how I'd broken his jaw. The jaw of the man I'd just fought with was definitely not broken. On the contrary, it was as sound a jaw as I'm ever likely to hit.

Now if I could remember what it was about that god-damned forearm of his. . .

I shelved these reflections while carrying, on legs still somewhat rubbery, Carol's suitcases out to the station wagon. I loaded up the back of the car, settled the kids in the back seat, and we took off. I slept again, awakening to the gaudy yellow sun-herald that is the Holiday Inn sign. "We are 'Mr. and Mrs. Peters' and children," Carol informed me as we walked into the office to register. I signed in while Carol kept Teddy and Emily at a safe range in case one of them should blurt out that I was not Mr. Peters but Uncle Dave.

We unpacked, I in my room, Carol and the kids in theirs, then I took them to the motel's restaurant for a family-style dinner. The kids did most of the eating; Carol poked morosely at her food and a splitting headache kept me off my diet. I had two bowls of split pea soup and quit.

The kids were falling off their feet when we returned to our rooms. I tucked them into the twin bed next to Carol's and told them a rather bewildering story about a giraffe who not only looked exactly like a zebra but was named Zebra as well—Zebra the Giraffe. Zebra meets this real zebra who looks exactly like a giraffe and is named Giraffe the Zebra. Fortunately, the kids fell asleep in the middle of it so I didn't have to sort it all out. Carol sat in a white quilted dressing gown, brushing her hair at a night table and watching me benignly in the mirror. Outside, the rain had diminished to a drizzle that hissed and pattered on the leaves.

"They have one of those first-run movie gadgets on the television set," I said. "Have you seen The Stepford Wives?"

"Yes."

"The other feature is Five Fingers of Death."

She brushed her hair to a high gloss. "Karate doesn't turn me on, exactly."

"There's a basketball game," I said, shuffling through a TV Guide.

"No."

"Movie of the Week?"

"No."

"Would you believe Marcus Welby? They've got a topnotch disease on tonight."

"No." She finished brushing her hair and gazed at me serenely.

I stood, rocking on my feet. "Don't you like television?"

"When there's nothing better to do."

"Look, Carol," I said, keeping my distance, afraid to approach her, "nothing has changed since the other night."

"That's true."

I fumbled with my fingers. "So. . . well. . . I guess I'll just knock off for the night. It's been a rough day."

"Yes," she said, passively, stoically.

I twiddled my fingers at her. "Well, good night now."

"Don't forget your scruples," she said.

"Got 'em right here," I said, tapping my heart.

I passed through the door that joined the two suites and closed it but hesitated over the lock. The act of bolting it was both simple and final and my motor responses seemed paralyzed. At last, I did it. The sound seemed thunderous to my ears. I flicked on the television set and sat down in a chair in front of it, not caring what came on. It was Marcus Welby. I stared at it stupidly, letting its prattle massage my aching head, but seeing nothing, recording nothing but the haunting image of Carol sitting forlornly in her room.

I think I passed a half-hour that way, a debate about duty versus desire raging around my brain. I wanted her desperately, and, client or no client, Jimmy Quinn seemed far, far away in time and space. Fixed games and murder and swindles didn't at that moment weigh a fraction of the weight of Carol's subtle perfume, balanced as the two were on the scales of reality.

I snapped off the television and went to my door. I could hear her brushing around preparing for bed. I began trembling with guilt. But not so much I couldn't unlock the door. I threw the bolt open and retreated to my bed, waiting.

A moment later the door opened and she stood there, diaphanous white nightgown flowing to a splash of chiffon around her feet. The glow from a bathroom light behind her exposed every contour of her body like a silhouette and highlighted her hair like a red aura.

"You asked for a rain check," I said.

She stepped up to me. "Yes."

I nodded toward the window. "It's raining."

"Yes," she said, raising the gown over her head and dropping it on the carpet.

Chapter IX

• • • •

I awoke with a headache and an erection. The headache was from the goon's forearm. The erection was from Carol's hand.

A pale pink pre-sunset light filtered through the curtains, and birds twittered outside, harbingers of a beautiful day.

"Before the kids get up. . ." she whispered, kissing me in the ear. I cupped her small buttocks and she rolled on top of me, thighs widespread. I slipped deeply into her and she whimpered with pleasure. Her hips undulated slowly, pushing the moist warm cavity as far as it would go, flexing the internal muscles around me like a velvet fist, then pulling away until I was on the verge of falling out of her, then ramming me home true again. It was like some new automotive concept whereby the piston remains stationary while the cylinder churns up and down.

She did this maddening thing to me for ten minutes, her breathing slow and controlled, working me until she knew I couldn't take another minute of it. Then she let herself go, quickening her pace. Her panting and sighing accelerated, her eyes began to roll and her lips to pout in ecstasy. We came together in perfect harmony, she in long rolling waves, I in immense spasms of relief.

We lay quietly a moment, coming down in stages from an incredible height. Then, abruptly, so abruptly it hurt me physically, she uncoupled from me and dashed into her room, shutting the door behind her. For a moment, I didn't understand. Then I heard a muffled, "Mommy?" Some maternal instinct had told her the kids were about to stir. I listened for a minute to the cheerful, chirpy dialogue of mother greeting children good morning. In an odd way, it saddened me, taking me back to a time of domestic happiness that had long ago been shattered, yet came back at times to haunt me, like today. Nancy and I had remained friends after the divorce, but not long ago had ruled out forever the possibility of reconciliation. I suppose it was a good thing, freeing both of us to start anew, and I had lately been dwelling on the desirability of remarrying, though there were no prospects near at hand. Certainly, I wasn't going to make much progress in that direction courting married women. Oh well. . .

I got out of bed a little too suddenly than was good for me and felt a pounding in my head and a nausea so strong I had to lean against the bathroom sink while brushing my teeth and shaving.

A knock on the door from Carol's side, then a pitter-patter of tiny feet and a swarm of small hands and kissing mouths.

"How do you feel this morning?" Carol said as if she hadn't seen me since early last evening. She leaned against the bathroom door, matronly in a flannel robe.

"Still a little punchy. I wonder if I could have my cranium set in a cast."

"A cup of coffee will do wonders."

"Prob—whoo boy!"

"What's the matter?"

"A cast! God bless Sigmund Freud!"

"What's he talking about, Mommy?" Teddy asked.

"Beats me," Carol shrugged. "What are you talking about?"

"A cast. The guy who broke into your house was wearing a cast on his arm. That's what he clobbered me with."

"So?" She handed me a towel as I rinsed the shaving cream off my face, noting in passing that between the lump on my brow from Midge and the one on my temple from last night's guy, my head must look like it was sprouting antennae.

"So?" I said, a little surprised at her obtuseness. "Who wears casts on their wrists?"

She looked at me as if the obtuseness were mine. "Why, anybody who breaks his wrist, I suppose."

"Football players, dummy!"

"My mommy's not a dummy," said Emily, kicking me on the ankle.

I picked her up and kissed her. "I was just calling myself a dummy for not thinking of it earlier." I shoved the kaboodle out of the wardrobe alcove for a moment while I dressed. "There were two Racer players whose initials match the ones on Jimmy's list," I said through the louvered double door. "One was Saul Talcott, the other Bucky Bradley. We can eliminate Talcott straight off because he's white. Bradley is black and he's a defensive tackle, the very kind of man you'd find wearing a cast on his forearm. He sure wielded it like he knew what he was doing."

I stepped out of the alcove, looking a lot more human than I felt. My misery was aggravated by having to play with the kids while Carol dressed but luckily I invented a game called Whisper which kept things on the placid side.

I took my little nuclear family to the coffee shop, and, as Carol had prognosticated, the coffee worked a minor miracle of healing. I looked at my watch and it was barely seven-thirty but it would not be long before the martinet-like Hobie Gilmore held his morning workout. "Where do the Racers practice?" I asked Carol.

"Indiana Central College, right here in Indianapolis. I can drive you over there."

"What time do they get underway?"

"Eight, usually. Gruesome hour. People shouldn't be asked to do anything athletic till three in the afternoon, at least."

"Oh, I don't know. Some folks awaken other folks at the crack of dawn for athletic activities," I smirked, asking for the check.

Carol dropped me off at the college campus, where a guard was fighting off a platoon of reporters clamoring for an interview with Hobie Gilmore. Silently, I cursed Roy Lescade again and shouldered my way through the throng. It was useless. The guard just took me for another reporter. "If Hobie knew I was out here, I guarantee he'd want to see me," I pleaded.

"Fifteen guys here say the same thing," the guard replied, leaning against the chicken-wire gate.

I tunneled out of the crush and stood on the perimeter, wondering what to do. Just then a lanky figure stepped out of a car and trotted toward the gate, carrying a large leather equipment bag. I recognized C. C. Tilden, one of the Racers' defensive ends. "I'm late," he snorted as I collared him.

"Please," I said. "Just tell Hobie Dave Bolt is out here and must see him. Will you remember?"

"Yeah, but I'm late," he said, yanking out of my grasp and barging through the reporters.

I had no faith Tilden would remember and I paced outside the gate contemplating bribery, tunneling, or armored assault. But after five minutes Tilden, in uniform, jogged over to the guard and said something to him, pointing at me. I burrowed into the wolf pack again and emerged inside, on a small football field glistening and muddy from last night's downpour. The offensive platoon was going through calisthenics under the south goal, the defensive under the north. Hobie was standing almost ankle deep in mud, oblivious to his own discomfort as he conferred with two assistants at a bridge table set up on the offense's side of the field.

I stood respectfully behind him, waiting to catch his attention. At length, he noticed me, excused himself, and strolled with me toward the gymnasium until we were out of earshot. His face was a purplish hue, only partially attributable to the chill of the early morning air.

"Who gave that story to that cocksucker?" he demanded, referring to Roy.

"I don't think anybody did, Hobie. I know Roy Lescade real well and I'm pretty certain he figured it out for himself. I third-degreed him yesterday and that's what he told me."

"You should have bashed his brains in. You know what it's done to the team?"

"I can imagine."

"It'll be a miracle if they can concentrate on football the rest of the week."

"Yes, sir. I told Roy we'd slap him with a libel suit."

"A lot of good that does me. The damage has been done. The Commissioner called me last night. He thought maybe I'd let the story leak. I thought he was going to flay me alive. Have you learned anything more?"

"Yes, I'm onto something, I don't want to talk about it yet. But I have to have a word with one of your players."

"Which one?"

"Bucky Bradley."

"Jesus, how is he mixed up in it?"

"I don't know if he is or not. I want to ask him some questions."

"Can't you tell me what it's all about? I've got fifteen torches under my ass and if I don't come up with some answers soon. . ."

I put my hand on his shoulder. "Hobie, I'm homing in, I swear, but I've got to ask for your tolerance just a little while longer."

He shook his head lugubriously, then turned and cupped his hands in the direction of the defensive squad. "Hey, Art? ART?"

Assistant defensive coach Art Claws looked over.

"Send Bradley over here!" Gilmore hollered.

A moment later an enormous figure separated itself from the knot of red-white-and-green jerseys and lumbered toward us, slogging through the mud like an infantryman. About halfway he flicked off his chin strap and removed his helmet and I looked at his right wrist.

It had a plaster cast on it.

He loomed before us, his number 72 spattered with mud, his face, a round beefy moon also dappled with mud, set in a natural sneer. He wore heavy, Clyde-like sideburns and mustache, but no goatee, affording me a look at his clean-shaven chin. It had a fresh cut on it an inch long and was slightly puffy. It was gratifying to know I'd at least drawn a little blood.

Since it had been dark in Carol's bedroom last night, he did not recognize me, but simply stared blankly, like a bull interrupted while pasturing.

"This gentleman would like to have a word with you," Hobie said. "Why don't you two go into the locker room?"

"What's it in reference to?" he said. It was the same baritone that had hurled oaths at me last night.

"Just go with the man; he'll explain," Hobie said, walking back to his bridge table.

I could feel tremors of suspicion and anxiety radiating from him as we squished through the sucking mud and pushed through the door to the locker room. I held the door for him and he clumped ahead of me down a rubber mat along a bank of lockers. I decided then and there that there was no better time to make my move. I kicked his rear foot into his front one just as it was coming off its stride and he fell heavily on his face. I leaped on his back and grabbed his right wrist, the broken one, and pretzeled him into a hammerlock before he could recover. Commando tactics compliments of the United States Army. I jerked his arm halfway up his spine, but his bicep was so big I couldn't push any farther and he was pushing back and kicking out trying to get a purchase on the floor. I grabbed a handful of wiry hair and thumped his head against the concrete floor, hard enough to smart, not hard enough to put him to sleep.

He twitched, then relaxed. "What you want, motherfucker?"

"I want to know why you broke into Jimmy Quinn's home last night?"

"Was that you?"

"Yeah, that was me."

"I thought I wiped your clock."

"Not enough. Answer my question."

"I was lookin' for sumpin'."

"What was it?"

"Money."

"You're a fuckin' liar. Look, Bucky. I know all about Jimmy's bankbook and that list. As a matter of fact, I have it, which is why you didn't find it. Now, suppose you tell me who sent you to take it?"

"No comment."

"You read the papers? You want to be named in a gambling scandal?"

"This ain't got nothin' to do with no gamblin' scandal, man."

"You want to tell that to the Commissioner? Baby, you could get thrown out of football so far you couldn't get in a sandlot game of touch on a Sunday afternoon. Now, who put you up to it?"

He breathed raspily, thinking it over. "Jimmy did."

"Jimmy Quinn?"

"Yeah. He called me after that story broke in the New York Post."

"Called you? From where?"

"From I don't know where, long distance, thass all."

"And said what?"

"And said I must get that list and savings book at all cost. He said if it got into the wrong hands, it could be misinterpreted. Just like you're doin'. Believe me, man, the list don't got shit to do with gamblin'. I swear to God."

I knew that already. "Did Jimmy say anything about that? About the gambling thing? About Al Negri's murder?"

"I asked him but all he said was, he'd straighten it all out when he come back."

"From where?"

"I tole you, I don't know. Long distance, thass all."

I sat on him, disappointed. I'd wandered into a blind alley, with nothing for my troubles but a bruised rib cage and a suspected hairline fracture of the skull. I jerked Bradley's arm to the breaking threshold. "You listen to me, motherfucker. You use that cast on anybody besides certified NFL offensive linemen, I'm gonna take after your balls with a pickax, do you read me, motherfucker?"

"Loud and clear, brother, loud and clear."

Chapter X

• • • •

I found a phone booth on the college campus and called Carol at the motel. She was to have called this friend of hers at the phone company to find out who owned the phone number penciled in the Quinn's address book under K. She'd succeeded. It belonged to a D. Pleasance at 900 Barnes Avenue.

It required considerably less detective skill than that of a Sherlock Holmes to deduce that D. Pleasance's name did not begin with a K and that the sex was probably female, marital status single, since many single women list only their first initial in order to discourage breathers and obscene callers.

A taxi ride of two minutes' duration took me to an apartment building of forty- or fifty-years' vintage with a rebuilt facade that looked like a lifted face on a wrinkled body. The doorman announced my name over the intercom, but despite the fact that my name meant nothing to the tenant of apartment 4B, the tinny voice, definitely female, ordered the fellow to admit me. The elevator ascended leisurely and I turned left as instructed.

The door of apartment 4B was open to the extent of its chain bolt and a platinum blonde bouffant with a person under it was looking out at me critically. "Did he say Dave Holt?" The voice was brassy with heavy Noo Yawk overtones.

"Dave Bolt," I corrected her.

"Are you RCA?"

"No, ma'am, NFL."

"What's that?"

"Just a little joke. I wanted to ask you some questions." I made out a puffy pale face, porcine eyes, acid green toreador pants, an extravagantly patterned green blouse tied over a bare midriff whose muscles were not as firm as one likes to see in bare midriffs.

"What kind of questions? Are you police?"

"No, nothing like that," I smiled, disarmingly I hoped. I didn't want to mention Kruger's name till I was in the door, fearful she might slam it in my face. For all I knew, Kruger was there.

"That's how the Boston Strangler got into women's apartments," D. Pleasance informed me.

I held out my palms. "Ma'am, do these look like the hands of a strangler?"

"Or you could be a rapist."

It was a tempting straight line but I fought back the obvious "Ma'am, does this look like the whang of a rapist?" I finally took a chance with, "It has to do with a Mr. Kruger."

"Oh." She closed the door a moment and I was about to kick myself but she'd done it only to unbolt the chain. The door opened wide, and I was faced with the remnant of a pretty woman dressed in a style that harked back to Chubby Checker and the Peppermint Lounge. I put her age at an old, worn, and tired forty-five. "I thought you were RCA for my television," she said. She had been imbibing the juice of the grape; a vile alcoholic odor emitted from her mouth.

"What's wrong with your television?"

"It doesn't work."

"Well, then, I'm afraid I can't help you. I'm good at on-off, volume, contrast, and channel selection, but after that you have to call an expert."

She looked me over and fluttered dark false eyelashes. "Will you have a drink, Mr. Holt?"

"It's Bolt and no thank you."

She gestured to a couch covered with plastic. I settled into it with an obscene squeak. She lit a cigarette and waved the smoke away. "What's this about Smiley? Have you heard from him?"

My heart dropped. Another blind alley and before I'd had a chance to ask her a single question. But I forged on. "No. Have you?"

"No, but I'm sure I will. How do you know him?"

"Uh, I have an investment with him."

"You too, huh? The Australian land bit?"

"Bit?" An interesting choice of words.

She shrugged. "Well, that's what he told me. He has this parcel of land in Australia he's gonna sell to these developers."

"And you believe him?"

"I hope to tell you. I've got twenty-five thousand dollars invested. Settlement from my second husband. Almost everything I have saved except some stock in Ford Motor Company and you might as well shove that up your giggy. Last time I looked at the financial page it was down to. . ."

"How do you know Smiley?" I asked.

"I met him on a cruise to Nassau."

"How well do you know him?"

She puffed frenetically on her cigarette and frowned. "What's that supposed to mean?"

"It's just that he gave me your name and address when I asked him where I could contact him," I said, lying facilely.

"He stays here when he's in town. Is that any crime?"

"No, no, no," I said defensively.

"He's my boyfriend, all right? I'm free, white, and twenty-one."

I found myself in agreement with two-thirds of that declaration. "I'm not here to pry about your relationship with Smiley," I said. "I'm just trying to locate him."

"Why? What's so urgent?"

"Aren't you urgently interested in what's become of your twenty-five thousand dollars?"

"Well. . . I'd have thought he'd call me by now. He usually calls me every couple of weeks whenever he's out of town. But I'm sure he's just tied up. He's probably in Australia."

"Does he have a home base? I mean, a permanent address?"

A flicker of the eyes told me she knew but her gaze crystallized to one of suspicion. She may have thought I was a cop or an enemy of Kruger's. "No," she said. "He just travels around a lot, that's all."

I looked hard at her, trying to penetrate her armor. "Has it ever occurred to you that this Australian bit is not strictly, uh. . ."

"Kosher?" I braced for an indignant reply but she continued, "Sure it's crossed my mind. But Smiley has always repaid my investments handsomely. He made me ten thousand on an investment of five a few months ago. Took him ten days, too. Australia is bigger, so it's taking a little longer. Besides, Smiley is. . . well, we've been seeing each other steadily. Whenever he's in Indianapolis, that is."

I choked down a smile. This woman was really being taken for a ride in a classic car and she didn't have an inkling. But I wanted to leave her with one, even at the risk of angering her. "You don't think it's possible he's been setting you up?"

"No way, Mr. Holt, not a chance." Her eyes, however, seemed clouded with a soupçon of doubt which she confirmed with, "But I'll tell you what. If I change my mind about that, I'll get in touch with you. You got a card or something?" I handed her my card and she studied it. "Oh, it's Bolt with a B?"

"Right. And if you hear from him, will you call me?"

"Sure."

A raucous buzzer sounded and she scurried to her intercom. "That's RCA."

"Make sure he has identification," I said. "It could be the Boston Strangler."

She smiled as she showed me to the front door. "Smiley will come back. I'm sure he will." I stepped into the corridor and she shut the door. As she did, I heard her mutter, "He'd better, the bastard."

I now found myself in another bottleneck. Unless I could get a line on Smiley Kruger, the likelihood of tracing Jimmy Quinn speedily was fainter than a star of the sixth magnitude. I wondered if Kruger's old club, the Colts, might have a record of their alumni's permanent addresses, or maybe the Commissioner's office kept them. I returned to the motel and called my office to instruct Trish and Dennis to follow up these hunches. What I got was Dennis's nearly hysterical "Dave! Thank God!"

"Dennis? Something the matter?"

"Well, how would you classify Trish's being arrested?"

I gasped. "As a practical joke?"

"Wrong."

"Arrested for what?"

"For harboring a fugitive from justice."

"A fugi—whoo boy. You mean, Rankin. . . uh, Rubin?"

"Rankin, Rubin, whatever the hell his name is."

"What happened, exactly?"

"Well, Trish and I were in the middle of lunch. . ."

"There, at the office?"

"Yeah. So, Gillian buzzes and says there are these two gentlemen outside from the FBI, asking for Trish. So I go out there to find out what's coming down, and here are these. . . boys. Dave, have you ever seen FBI agents? They look like choirboys. Whatever happened to—?"

"What happened then?"

"They flash this warrant. I told them Trish wasn't here. They said, 'Unless she's jumped out the window, we happen to know she is here.' Trish came out and they read her her rights and whipped her on down to the U.S. Court House in Foley Square."

"What happened to Rubin?"

"Oh yeah. She asked if she could make one phone call and they said, 'If it's to your boyfriend Rubin, forget it. We got him an hour ago.' Dave, are you laughing?"

"Just smiling a little. I don't know why, I really feel like crying but the thought of Trish being booked—"

"I feel the same way. But we gotta do something."

"Did you call Byron?" Byron Seltzer was our attorney.

"Yeah. He's on his way down there now. I don't think he'll have much trouble springing her."

"Whatever it costs—"

"Of course. What about Rubin?"

"Let him make his own arrangements. No, wait a minute, I have an idea.'

"What's that?"

"Well, put it this way, if you get a call from Roy Lescade about this, cooperate with him to the fullest extent."

"I thought you weren't speaking to him."

"I wasn't. Now I am. Find out what they set Rubin's bail at. I know he's got family here and maybe they can foot the bill themselves. If not, we're going to put the money up. Preferably, with a big splash of publicity."

"Any other instructions?"

"Yeah. I'm urgently trying to find the last permanent address of Smiley Kruger. Remember him?"

"Sure. Baltimore Colts, 1960. . . uh. . . let's see, Unitas joined the club in. . ."

"Just find out where I can reach him."

"How important is this?"

"More important than getting Trish out of jail."

"You cruel bastard."

"Let her cool her ass in the Federal House of Detention for a couple of hours. It can only do her good."

"Shall I tell her you said that?"

"Do that and you'll never see another sunrise."

I hung up and placed a call immediately to Roy Lescade. As I waited to be put through, I practiced swallowing my pride. It stuck in my throat like a horse pill.

I held the line while Roy finished talking to somebody, then he clicked on. "Roy, it's Dave."

He seemed to be pausing to catch his breath. "Well, well. I figured next time I heard from you, it would be from your second asking me time, place, and weapons for a duel."

"That's still a distinct possibility," I said. "But something's come up, another story. I thought you'd like to have an inside track on it."

"Aha! Decided it's easier to catch flies with honey, have you?"

"Yeah. I figured you might get bored with a steady diet of cowshit."

"What's the story?"

I ran down the Bob Rubin saga for him, capping it with the arrest of Rubin and Trish. He listened attentively, interrupting me occasionally to ask for a detail or a correct spelling and I could hear him scratching his notes on a pad.

When I finished, he said, "Now, that's my kind of story."

"That's what I figured."

"What's in it for you?"

"I need to enlist public sympathy for Rubin. If the sentiment is, 'The kid's suffered enough, leave him alone,' there's a chance the government will give him a break."

"That sentiment may be harder to come by than you think, buddy. A lot of people regard these holdouts as pigheaded fanatics. And if you think I'm gonna paint a bleeding-heart picture of Rubin. . ."

"I've never dictated the content of your stories, Roy. You print what you have to print."

"I'll get down to the Court House right away. Does this mean we're friends again?"

"Fuck no!" I said, hanging up.

Chapter XI

••••

Carol looked distressed as we stopped before the security barrier of the airport. She'd have looked even more so if she hadn't had to cast anxious glances at the kids, who were standing in the newspaper concession debating which candies to buy with the quarters I'd given them.

She had good reason to be unhappy as it was the second time in three days I'd taken leave of her abruptly. But between the crisis in New York and the blind alley I'd run into on Smiley Kruger's whereabouts, there was no point in hanging around Indianapolis. But I consoled her with the assurance that I was bending every resource at my disposal toward locating Kruger.

Frankly, the assurance was probably more consoling to her than to me. It wasn't merely that I doubted finding Kruger, it was that I doubted finding him before Jimmy Quinn did. When that happened, only a few things could transpire, every one of them equally appalling to contemplate. Furthermore, I had a deadline. If Jimmy failed to show up for Sunday's game, now only three days away, everything Roy had implied in his Post article would be confirmed and the fallout from this particular mushroom cloud could contaminate professional football from coast to coast.

At the moment, my best chance of finding Kruger lay with his Indianapolis girlfriend—for I'm sure he had one in every port—Dolores Pleasance. I uttered this reflection aloud, to which Carol responded with, "You really think she knows where he is?"

"I really do but she's protecting him. She is certain she's his one-and-only and that he's coming back with a treasure chest filled with greenbacks and then he'll marry her. I tried to plant some doubts in her skull but I don't think they penetrated her bouffant."

She looked pensively past me, through the tunnel of the metal detector at the swarms of travelers hustling to and from boarding gates 8 through 16. Some kind of internal turmoil was causing her brows to squinch together like contracting muscles trying to give birth to an idea. Then she licked her upper lip and said, "There must be some way we can disabuse dear old Dolores of her notion that Smiley is coming back for her."

"Time will do that, except we don't have any."

"Then we have to force it," she said.

"Yes, but how to do that, unless. . .?"

I believe the idea came to both of us at once. Carol articulated it first. "Unless I pay her a visit. . ."

". . . pretending to be a girlfriend of Smiley's who's looking for him!" I completed the sentence with snapping fingers. "Do you think you can do it?"

Her eyes brightened as she pictured herself performing the role. "Yes, I'm sure of it. I've had a lot of practice playing the abandoned woman."

I looked at my watch and picked up my bag "You'll have an opportunity to rehearse right now. I'm afraid it's time to go." I took her hand, cordially for public consumption. But I pressed it with a secret message of affection. "Good luck in your acting debut."

"I'll call you after our tête-à-tête."

Despite a tailwind, the plane couldn't get to New York fast enough to suit me. Nor could the taxi from LaGuardia Airport, zipping up the Van Wyck Expressway against the coarse grain of rush-hour traffic out of Manhattan, hit the Triboro Bridge quickly enough; nor could the elevator in the Lincoln Building soar fast enough to the 18th floor, though I was its only passenger.

My office had more people in it than it had ever held except the time the graduating seniors of a college basketball team had come to me asking me to represent them as a unit so they could continue playing ball together. My eyes immediately darted to Trish, who held a tall drink and seemed not a stitch the worse for her ordeal. Surrounding her, also holding drinks tinted suspiciously the color of my special reserve of Wild Turkey, were Dennis Whittie, Roy Lescade, my attorney Byron Seltzer, a black girl I'd never seen before, and my English receptionist Gillian.

It was certainly an odd array, the kind you can only see at a New York gathering. Byron, straight and proper as always in his immaculate three-hundred-dollar three-piece lawyer suit with subdued Sulka tie of fabulous silk, hobnobbed with the black girl garbed in spangled blue faded jeans, a red silk blouse flowing over small braless breasts, a fur vest stripped off the carcass of what appeared to have been an Airedale and a hairdo composed of those tightly twisted, licorice-stick-like strands known as corn-rows. Dennis, cool in his white wool slacks, high-heeled shoes, qiana shirt slashed to the belly and shark's tooth suspended by a silver chain from his neck, rapped with Roy, who not surprisingly looked like he'd just finished cleaning a septic tank with his raincoat while still wearing it. Gillian stood outside the knot of people, shy, aloof, awkward, and possibly stupid. I am so totally in love with English accents that it frequently takes me years to discover that the owner of one is a low-grade moron. Gillian was hardly that but when it came to sports, she was close. She knew less than diddly about them and was perpetually embarrassing me by addressing baseball players as "batters" and football linemen as "forwards."

Trish caught my eye and plunged out of the crowd for a relieved embrace, sloshing her drink down my neck. "Oh, Dave, you wouldn't believe. . ."

I hugged her tightly. 'I'd believe it."

"I mean, I was busted in a peace demonstration a couple of years ago but that was a day in the country compared to this. This was scary. This was big-time, real-life, big-people scary. Give me a red-necked Cracker cop any day over these apple-cheeked Federal gentlemen-sadists." She stepped away and peered at the bruise on my temple. "Now what? Another elevator accident?"

"No, I got plastered. Only, the plaster had set when the guy hit me with it."

"Your head is beginning to look like a golfball."

"People seem to have been mistaking it for one lately."

She hooked my arm and pulled me into the room. I took in the faces as a clamor of greetings went up. "I know everyone but you," I said to the black girl, who upon closer inspection was less a girl than a young woman and one with intense, shrewd dark eyes that seemed to zoom in on where my head had been at the moment they fixed me.

"This is Gartha Wilcoxon," Trish said. I held out my hand for a conventional shake but when Gartha's thumb extended vertically, I switched to the revolutionary salute, twining my thumb around hers and pressing my forearm to her wrist.

"Hello, sister," I said.

"Mr. Bolt." Her voice was sharp and commanding.

"And you are. . .?"

"Bob Rubin's attorney," she replied.

Everyone's eyes were riveted to my face, amusedly waiting for my astonished reaction. I tried to deprive them of the pleasure by responding like Mister Cool but you really could have knocked me over with a feather, and I'd have had to be cooler than the Blue Grotto to prevent my eyes from widening involuntarily and my lips from parting for a sibilant intake of air.

"They're turning lawyers out in all colors these days, Mr. Bolt," she said, quietly rejoicing in my confusion.

"It wasn't your color but your beauty," I said resorting to the kind of gallant flattery that had made my male ancestors as unprincipled a dynasty of cads as ever seduced fair maidens. "They don't turn out many lawyers as easy on the eyes as you."

"Barf," said Roy Lescade, who knew a line of blarney when he heard one. "And what's with the revolutionary handshake, you hypocrite? Last time I heard, you were slightly to the right of the Buckley family."

I ignored the remark and looked around the room as Trish produced a drink and pressed it into my hand. "Well?" I addressed the company at large. "What're we gonna do?"

"We were just standing around waiting on you, O Mighty Leader," said Dennis.

I shrugged. "I guess the first order of business is for everybody to have another round of drinks. Maybe we'll all get so pie-eyed we won't have to cope with this mess till tomorrow."

Gartha flashed me an unappreciative look so I had no choice but to turn solemn and get down to cases. "What about Bob Rubin? Has he been released?"

"The magistrate hasn't fixed bail yet," Gartha replied. "The matter'll have to carry over till tomorrow. But it won't carry over a minute more or I'm gonna have that judge's ass."

"I trust you phrased that threat a bit more diplomatically when you addressed His Honor today," I remarked, looking over at Byron, who was a lot closer to my idea of what a lawyer is supposed to look like.

He smiled jovially. "You don't have to worry about her, Dave. She's an extremely competent attorney."

"I'm sure the magistrate loved the nail heads on her blue jeans," Roy chuckled. I held back a smile but I really had to hold with Roy. It was a little hard for me to conceive of this gal pleading a case before a magistrate dressed like that. In fact, most judges I know wouldn't let an attorney into their chambers dressed like that.

"I wasn't wearing this when I appeared before Neuberger," she said defensively. Then her eyes roved over Roy's disheveled and stained clothes and she added, "Besides, you're not exactly the glass of fashion."

That broke up the room and I decided I really liked this little firebrand.

"Okay," I said, "tomorrow Neuberger fixes bail on Bob Rubin. Unless it's astronomical, I'll put up the money myself." This elicited a surprised look from Trish, and I looked back at her with a gaze that expressed our private understanding. "I am, after all, Bob Rubin's agent. Then, we have to prepare Bob's defense. The trouble is, and with all due respect to Bob's able counsel, I can't see a conventional defense working. The government's case is cut and dried and no amount of anti-war rhetoric will sway a judge who's got to decide the case on purely legal merits. So, we've got to put some pressure on the government to drop its case or mitigate its charges or recommend leniency. Now, I have some ideas about that, too, but I'll entertain some suggestions from the floor."

"I'd like to call Gary Albert of the Jets," Trish said, referring to the team's general manager. "I want to know if he's still going to be interested in Bob once he knows who Bob really is."

"You can try," I said, "but what's Albert going to say? He can't make that decision until he knows the Commissioner's position. The Commissioner must, after all, rule as to the league's attitude toward a would-be player who has blatantly broken the law of the land."

"Then we'll go to the Commissioner," Trish said.

"Yes," I sighed, "but what's he gonna say? Most likely, that his hands are tied and he won't be able to take a stand until he knows the outcome of the trial. Besides," I added with a withering look at Roy, "I'm in somewhat bad odor with the Commissioner at the moment, thanks to the untimely release of a calumnious story about Jimmy Quinn in a certain newspaper."

Trish, her complexion ashen, leaned heavily against my desk. "I can see what's shaping up. Everyone's going to pass the buck and Bob will end up getting the shaft."

An almost intolerably heavy blanket of gloom descended over us and Roy's feeble "Well, maybe my story in tomorrow's paper will help" did very little to dispel it. It was all well and good to publicize the case but publicity alone wouldn't achieve any miracles. What we needed was some political muscle. Besides, as Roy had hinted, there was no guaranteeing his story would be completely sympathetic to Rubin.

Everyone in the room focused on Roy and impaled him on the lance of a dirty look. For if Roy had held back that article on Jimmy Quinn, I wouldn't be on the Commissioner's shit-list for withholding information and impeding his investigation. Then I'd have been able to go to him and ask him as a favor to put his weight behind Bob Rubin's defense. He might not have obliged me but at least I'd have been free to ask. As things stood, to ask the Commissioner a favor at this time, when the sight of me would probably make him purple with rage, would be an act requiring more nerve than this poor old soul ever hoped to possess.

"What's everybody lookin' at me for?" Roy snarled, helping himself to a glass full of bourbon and quaffing it with his back turned to us.

Now, I don't pretend to be any more religious than the next person; my daddy liked to say, "Pray for a good harvest but work the fields sixteen hours a day anyway." At this point, only something resembling a miracle would have helped us out of our bind and I wasn't counting on one. Which is why, when the phone rang, I snapped at Gillian, "I don't want to talk to anybody except God."

Gillian picked up in the reception room, argued with someone for a minute, then hung up while we debated some aspects of Bob Rubin's case. Gillian came back into the room and took her place at the perimeter, looking complaisant, like a cow.

"Who was that?" I asked.

"A Mrs. Pleasance," she replied. "She said it was rather important and would like you to call her. . ."

"You hung up on her?" I exclaimed.

"You said you didn't want to talk to anybody," she said fretfully and righteously.

"Anybody except God is what I said."

"I beg your pardon?"

"Never mind. What's her number? Get her for me."
Gillian, all afluster, scurried into the reception room and
punched out the ten digits of Dolores Pleasance's number.
I looked at the puzzled faces in the room. "Sorry, fellas
and gals, but this may be the break we need. Excuse me."

I went into Trish's office next door, watching Gillian on
the phone. She listened, spoke a few words, then raised her
eyes in my direction. "Ready with your call, Mr. Bolt, on 41."

I closed the door behind me, picked up the receiver and
punched the 41 button. "Hello?"

"Mizzter Bolt," Dolores Pleasance slurred into the
phone. She had obviously had a tankful.

"Mrs. Pleasance, what a nice surprise!"

"You, too," she said in something less than a sequitur.

"What can I do for you?"

"You can get that fucking bazztid for me. And my
money, the fucking bazztid."

"You mean Kruger?" I said, playing it straight.

"Who else would I mean, you goddamn fool?"

I absorbed the insult soundlessly. "What made you
change your mind?" I asked, silently blessing Carol Quinn.

"It's a woman's prerogative, isn't it? I'm free, white,
and twenty-one aren't I?"

"Yes, ma'am."

"Well, then, that's all you have to know. I just decided
that fucking bazztid wasn't coming back with my money.
He's probably spending it on some cheap floozie this very
minute, the fucking bazztid. 'Scuse me while I light a
drink. I mean a cigarette." The phone banged noisily five
or six times against a wall as it swung free and I could
hear Dolores muttering in the background. I gripped the
receiver with white knuckles, fearful she'd pass out before

she could get back to the phone. Finally, she came back on. "You there, sweetie?"

"I'm here, ma'am."

"Awright. You ever hear of Manzanillo?"

"In Mexico?"

"No, in New Rochelle, you big goddamn jerk. Of course, in Mexico!"

"Well, then, I've heard of it."

"He's got a villa down there, it's called Las Something-or-other."

"Can you tighten that up a little, Mrs. Pleasance? 'Las' covers quite a lot of territory."

"Umm. Las. . . Las. . . it's a girl's name, but also a flower, he once told me that, the fucking bazztid."

"Las Rosas?"

"No."

"Las Margaritas?"

"Hey, yes! That was terrific. How'd you do that?"

"I grew up with Mexicans. Margaritas are daisies."

"Right. Well, that's it. It's on a big road in the hills over the town, El Camino Something-Something."

"I'll find it," I said.

"I'll give you twenty-five percent of whatever you recover, plus, if you kick his balls in, I'll give you another twenty-five percent, the fucking bazztid. And if you tear her hair out, whoever she is, the goddamn bitch. . ."

"I'll do what I can, ma'am," I said.

I hung up just as a second phone rang, lighting up the 40 button. On a hunch, I punched it.

"Dave?"

"Carol!"

"Hi. Listen, I paid Dolores Pleasance a visit and I think I put a bug in her ear, so if she calls you. . ."

"She already did and she told me where I can find Kruger."

"Fantastic!"

"You're fantastic! I'm nominating you for an Oscar. What did you say to the lady?"

"Oh, I told her how Smiley had sweet-talked me out of my life's savings two years ago. . . I even burst into tears." More solemnly, she said, "I told you—I've had a lot of practice. Where is Kruger?"

"In a village in Mexico. Actually, not a village any more since some tin magnate erected a resort there."

"Do you think Jimmy's there?"

"I dearly hope so because my neck is in a noose and the hangman's about to kick my horse out from under me." She lapsed into a long silence filled with the interference of long-distance noises, bleeps and crackles and shreds of fascinating conversations.

Finally, she brought it out. "I guess I hope so, too."

"You guess. . .?"

"Dave, you really are obtuse."

"That's the second time in two minutes someone's suggested I'm stupid."

"I'm sorry, I thought you'd understand."

"If you meant you don't want our affair to end, I understood perfectly well, but. . ."

"Don't say it."

". . . it's unrealistic for us to think we can. . ."

"Please don't say it. Please!"

"It's going to have to be said sooner or later," I sighed.

"Then say it later. I haven't had enough of you, Dave. I lie awake at night, alone in my bed, and all I can think of. . ."

"Carol, don't," I begged her.

"I just want you a little while longer."

I really didn't know how to answer her. The prospects

for our romance had receded as sharply as the prospects of finding Jimmy had advanced. I'd already made up my mind to leave for Mexico at once—tonight, if possible. If I found him, if I brought him back, the exquisite bubble of my affair with his wife would burst. She obviously cared more than a little for me and I wasn't exactly indifferent to her but what was I supposed to do? Hope I found him dead? Hope he went to jail? Even if he were a perfect stranger, common decency, of which I do have a vestige, believe it or not (it's just that sometimes I forget where I put it), would dictate that I urge Carol to try for a reconciliation with her husband. But Jimmy was no mere common stranger. He was a client and no small-potatoes client, either. I'd broken one of my most cherished principles, to say nothing of one of the Ten Commandments and if I didn't end the thing now it could prove catastrophic. But I couldn't chop it down cleanly. "Why don't we just wait and see," I said, trying to avoid the subject.

"See what? See Jimmy return for one night and then go off chasing his groupies again? Dave, if I thought you'd wait for me, I'd start divorce proceedings tomorrow."

I grimaced. "Hey now, that's a little heavy!"

"The kids adore you."

"That's an infatuation. First time I hollered at them, they'd start screaming for their daddy back."

"I won't live with him the way we've been living. Just one night with you convinced me of that."

"Well, then, maybe I've served my purpose. Can't you let it go at that?"

"I don't want to. But you do, don't you?"

"I think you owe your husband another chance."

"Yes, but doesn't he owe me something, too?"

"Tell him."

Her voice picked up firmness. "Oh, I will, in no uncertain terms. But if he takes me lightly this time—well, don't be surprised one day to find a mother and two children camped on your doorstep."

All this was assuming Jimmy came back safe and sound. That unspoken thought passed between us like the shadow of a monstrous bird. At length, I said, "I've got to get back to my guests."

"At least say you're a little bit crazy about me."

It wasn't difficult to comply with her request.

I walked back to my office to find the gang pretty much frozen in the attitudes in which I'd left them, chattering idly. The susurration ceased abruptly as I crossed the threshold. My guests seemed to sense that no ordinary thing had happened.

"Okay," said Roy, "who is Dolores Pleasance?"

"Buddy, you are the last person in the world I would tell who Dolores Pleasance is. Suffice it to say, she may just have pointed the way to the answer to our prayers."

Naturally, everyone began showering me with questions but I held up my hands and said, "Sorry, folks, I can't talk about it. Best thing for now is for us all to disperse and do our own things. Roy, you got a story to write. Gartha, you spring Bob Rubin from the hoosegow tomorrow. Trish'll draw the bail money as soon as we know what it's gonna cost. Trish, make a date with Gary Albert of the Jets and sound him out about Bob Rubin. Byron?"

My attorney looked up at me.

"You got Trish's case to prepare."

"Right."

"What's our defense, counselor?"

"Simply that Trish was not cognizant of 'Bob Rankin's' true identity when she put him up in her apartment. I'm making a motion for dismissal on those grounds tomorrow. The government hasn't an iota of evidence. I expect Neuberger'll throw the case out tomorrow. They don't want Trish. They just wanted to punish her a little."

"For what?"

Byron laughed, exchanging glances with Trish. "Well, she kind of gave the FBI agents a rough time, called them some names, kneed one in the. . . um. . . groin. The agent told me he hadn't heard language like that since Marine boot camp."

I looked sternly at Trish, but it was no use—I had to grin. "Trish, Trish, Trish."

"What can I tell you?" Trish shrugged. "The sonofabitch felt me up while he was frisking me."

Dennis stepped forward. "You need me?"

"Yes. Stick around. Gillian, you too."

Gillian looked at her watch and made an audible sigh. I love these English secretaries—all dedication from nine to five but God help you if you ask them to put in one minute's overtime. "Am I inconveniencing you?" I asked her pointedly.

"No, that's all right," she said, saccharinely conveying the opposite.

The meeting disbanded, with Dennis and Gillian hanging back in my office. "Gillian, find out what connections I can make either tonight or early tomorrow to Manzanillo, Mexico. It's about a fifty-minute flight out of Mexico City on Aeromexico. Book me on the first plane to Mexico City that'll enable me to make that Manzanillo hop. But I don't want to hang around Mexico City so keep the connections tight."

"Yes, Mr. Bolt."

She glided out of the room almost on wheels; put a vial of acid on her head and she wouldn't have spilled a drop. Gillian was perfect. I think I hated her.

"Dennis, you think the Commissioner is still in?"

He looked at his watch and held his palms out. "Possibly. He puts in pretty long hours."

"Would you call him and tell him I'd like to see him right away?"

"I don't know if His Highness will grant you an audience. He's pretty sore at you."

"Tell him I have. . . um. . . news of a possibly dramatic breakthrough. Use that phrase, 'News of a possibly dramatic breakthrough.'"

"'News of a possibly dramatic breakthrough.' I'm impressed, at least. Should I say anything about the Bob Rubin thing?"

"No, I'll take that up with him when I see him."

"Fine."

He went into his office just as Gillian was returning, notepad dark with shorthand jottings. "There are no flights to Manzanillo after ten P.M. and you couldn't possibly be in Mexico City in time to catch the last one. As you don't wish to lay over in Mexico City tonight, I've booked you on Aeromexico flight 118 out of Kennedy International leaving nine tomorrow morning, arriving approximately twelve-thirty Mexico time, in time to catch the one o'clock flight to Manzanillo. Your tickets will be waiting at the Aeromexico desk tomorrow morning. It's suggested you arrive—"

"That'll be fine, Gillian."

"You're allowed forty-five pounds—"

"That'll be fine, Gillian."

". . . typhoid vaccination. . ."

"Gillian. . ."

". . . passport. . ."

"Gillian, Goddamnit!"

She came to attention. "Yes, Mr. Bolt?"

"I admire excellence in all things but if you serve me

any more thoroughly, I'll fire you."

She looked at me blankly but I could see she was savoring her petty little vengeance. "Shall you be needing me any further, sir?"

"No, I shan't."

"Ta ta, then. Enjoy your trip." She pivoted smartly and glided soundlessly out of the room. A moment later the outer door clicked behind her and a moment after that Dennis strode into the room, lips pursed. That usually meant an aborted mission "The Commissioner wasn't in, right?" I said, anticipating.

"No, he was in, but he said he was going to be tied up in conference for some time to come and he can't break it."

"Did you tell him. . .?"

"Yeah, 'News of a possibly dramatic breakthrough.'"

"And what did he say?"

"He said he has an assistant who can handle the matter just as well. I wasn't sure if you wanted to or not so I told him we'd get back. What do you say?"

"I don't talk to underlings when I can help it."

"That's what I figured."

"Did he say who the assistant was?"

"Yeah, someone named Posner."

I smiled. "Call back and say I'll be delighted to get together with Mr. Posner."

Dennis's face twitched. "Dave, I must confess I don't always understand where you're at."

"That's what's made me the greatest sports agent on the eighteenth floor of the Lincoln Building," I said.

Chapter XII

· · · ·

The National Football League is headquartered at 410 Park Avenue, about a ten-minute walk from my office. It's relatively squat as Park Avenue office buildings go and completely devoid of architectural merit, an insult to the gorgeous Lever House a block south of it or the Seagram Building two blocks southeast of it. The Seagram Building is a soaring monolith sheathed in bronze oxidized to a brown so dark it's all but black. It's set back from Park Avenue by a spacious fountained plaza with low walls on which pedestrians and office workers sit and cool their heels, eat brown-bagged lunches and, to use the Yiddish word Trish taught me, "shmooze" with one another while watching the passing scene. I stopped there and though it was a chilly evening, I sat down for a moment to draw my thoughts together and sharpen the sword with which I was about to do battle with Barry Posner. Then I moved on.

A lone guard sat in the lobby of 410 Park, staring into the darkness, presiding over the visitors' list with complete indifference.

The elevator catapulted me to the 12th floor where I stepped into a reception area so stark and featureless it reminded me of the anteroom of an insurance company except even insurance companies offer you reading matter. In order to enter, you have to petition a receptionist sequestered behind a three-foot-high wall topped with another three or four feet of thick glass. She will then buzz you through a door if your credentials are in order and your appointment legitimate. At this hour there was no receptionist and it took five minutes of glass-tapping with a coin to attract the attention of Barry Posner in the inner sanctum. Posner came out looking at me like I'd just smeared doggie-poo on the plate-glass window and reached under the receptionist's desk to buzz me through. We did not shake hands. I followed him into the inner rooms whose austerity never ceased to shock me considering the color and pageantry of the sport the office represented. One of these days, I was going to recommend to the Commissioner that he bring in my ex-wife, an interior decorator, to pump some sex appeal into these precincts.

Posner's office was as barren as a jail cell and we glared at each other across the white light of a Tensor lamp whose neck was cocked like a bantam rooster's over his paperless desk.

"I understand you have something for us," he said.

"Well, actually I wanted to speak to the Commissioner, but I guess you'll do almost as well." I dislike myself when I get petty, but I also forgive myself when the object is an officious little subaltern like Posner.

"Would you like to state your business? It's late and I've put in a long day."

"Yes. I have the solution to the Jimmy Quinn mystery."

"Do you have Jimmy Quinn himself?"

"I'll know that in a day or two."

"A day or two is all we have, Bolt. The excuses we've been handing out about Quinn's absence are thinner than tissue. Your friend's story in the Post has placed us in an intolerable position. The only way we can combat the criticism and ward off a formal investigation is to produce Jimmy Quinn by Sunday. We would like to know the solution to the mystery but it's secondary in our priorities. What we want, to state it unequivocally, is Jimmy Quinn by Sunday afternoon, in condition to play. Play well, play poorly, that's of no concern to us as long as he is there for the world to see."

"You couldn't make yourself clearer."

"You still haven't stated your business."

"I want to offer you a deal."

"What kind?"

"If I deliver Quinn by Sunday. . ."

Posner removed his horn-rimmed glasses and leaned over his desk combatively. I was surprised at his belligerence but he looked as if he required only the slightest additional provocation to leap over the top and assault me. I wouldn't have thought him capable of physical mayhem, especially considering I could make liverwurst out of him with both hands tied behind my back. The fact that he was indifferent to this is a tribute to the intensity of his rage. "Bolt, if you're harboring Quinn for some reason, so help me, I'll see to it that you're. . ." He sputtered threats of blackballing me, of having me indicted on a variety of counts, and of personally thrashing me. I can't remember when I've so thoroughly enjoyed watching a man blow his cool.

"I don't have him," I said calmly. "I just reckon I may have him directly. Of course, I'm not in quite as big a rush as you are. If I find him Monday, Tuesday, it's not gonna bug me same as it bugs you. But I could give it the old college try in exchange for some help I need with another problem."

"The problem of Bob Rubin?"

I scratched my nose. "Ah, you know about that already?"

"Bolt, when are you going to learn? A sparrow doesn't fall in the National Football League that we don't know about. We knew of Rubin's impending arrest before it happened. Hell, we've known Rubin's identity for three years. Why don't you close your mouth before something flies into it?"

He was right. My jaw was hanging limply in wonder. "How come you never said anything?"

"What business was it of ours?"

"True."

"But when the Jets and other NFL teams started courting Rubin, then it became our business."

Suddenly I had a thought, and a gallon of angry adrenaline sluiced into my bloodstream. I got to my feet and leaned over the desk, my face an inch away from Posner's "Did you turn Rubin over to the FBI, you little bastard?"

He hung in there, gazing directly back into my eyes for a moment to show me he wasn't afraid of me. "Why would I do that?"

"To get even with me. To flush the special dope I have on Jimmy Quinn into the open. To force me to deal with you."

He pushed his chair on rollers back to the wall. "Well, I think I'll leave you to wonder about it. Maybe you'll come out of this with a little more respect for this office. Now, how can we be of help to you with the Bob Rubin affair?"

My fury subsided and I dropped back into my seat, looking at this worthy adversary with grudging admiration. This was one of the keenest minds I'd ever dealt with and one of the cruelest. I'd walked into this meeting with cocky confidence that I was forcing Posner to play my game. Now, it appeared he'd been in control all along. But the injury was mainly to my vanity, for when all was said and done, I was still in a position to dictate terms. Well, that's not quite true, I was in a position to request them. And if I said Please often and respectfully enough, I just might get my way. "I'd like the government to drop its case against Rubin. Do you think that's possible?"

"No. But we might be able to prevail on the government to entertain a compromise."

"What sort of compromise?"

"I'm not ready to discuss that."

"When will you be?"

"When I turn on my television set Sunday and see Jimmy Quinn calling plays for the Indianapolis Racers."

"Can you at least tell me what the Commissioner's attitude is toward Bob Rubin? Is he sympathetic, unsympathetic?"

Posner rolled forward and put his elbows on the desk. "Bolt, have you given me any reason to want to make you feel comfortable?"

"I reckon not."

"Well, then, don't ask questions I'm not going to answer. You want relief from your anxieties, you know what you have to do." He stood up, bringing our interview to a close with a silence louder than the crack of a gavel.

I found my way out and stepped into the elevator. "Well," I said aloud as the doors glided shut in front of me, "I guess I put him in his place!"

Chapter XIII

• • • •

About two-thirds of the way up the Pacific coast between Acapulco and Puerto Vallarta lies Manzanillo. For a couple of centuries, its main industry was fishing and except for an occasional tidal wave from a shift of the Circum-Pacific Earthquake Fault, nothing ever happened there. Then a man named Patiño, heir to a Bolivian tin-mining fortune, fixed on Manzanillo as the ideal location for a sumptuous resort and that was it for Manzanillo. The resort is named Las Hadas, which means "The Fairies" in Spanish. I'm not sure why it was named that, the long-legged bronze-skinned women striding across the pink-beige sand of the beach in their "string" bikinis provide ample reassurance that sharp demarcation between sexes still exists in some parts of the world—and in Manzanillo, with a vengeance.

Perhaps it's the somewhat fey architecture, with its turrets and towers and stucco villas of blinding white and the mosaic-patterned cobblestone streets (from which gas-oline-driven cars are banished in favor of electric carts, by the way). Instead of conventional cabañas, they have gaily colored Bedouin tents and the whole impression is so Saracen that a Christian fears a little for his head as he checks into the hotel.

After settling into my incredibly luxurious balconied room with its Italian marble tub that beckoned this weary traveler to his doom (I'd spend two hours in it and fall asleep for six more when I got out), I returned to the lobby and secured a map of the town and outlying area from a delicious almond-eyed Mexican tour hostess who arranged for me to pick up a car from the Avis lot beyond the hotel's pale, where internal combustion engines were permitted. According to the map, the main residential road in the hills above the town was El Camino de los Pescadores ("The Road of the Fishermen") and I suspect that was what Dolores Pleasance, in her alcoholic stupor, was thinking of when she tried to remember the location of Smiley Kruger's villa, Las Margaritas. My hostess batted long lashes at me and said she thought Las Margaritas was to be found on Pescadores, but she wasn't exactly sure. She obligingly went to a directory for me and confirmed that I would indeed find it there, probably two or three miles up the winding road into the lush green-terraced hills above the seaport.

I asked her if she had registered here or had seen the likes of, one Jimmy Quinn. Negative answers to both which didn't surprise me. I doubted if Jimmy could afford half an hour in this hotel, where I was paying $108 a day, meals excluded, for the privilege of checking my suitcase. The environs were replete with smaller hotels and inns that had sprung up in the shadow of Las Hadas and Jimmy was probably holed up in one if he hadn't already made contact with Kruger. It wasn't worth doing a house-to-house search for Jimmy; I suspected that when I found Kruger, I'd find Jimmy, too. The critical question was, in what condition would I find him?

Avis offered me a choice of Volkswagens, including garishly decorated The Things, or American cars. I selected a Buick Skyhawk, compact for rough mountain roads but powerful enough to chase or be chased if it came to that. I didn't want to be caught short in a putt-putt if push should come to shove, as push seemed to have done with growing frequency in my life lately.

I drove south through the old town and beyond it, along the coast road commanding the azure Pacific. The sky was cloudless except for some immense pink thunderheads far, far off on the horizon, too far to affect local weather, but I knew that within an hour the late afternoon breeze would shift off the land, magically producing black clouds and perhaps torrential rains before just as magically dispersing.

A couple of minutes out of town, I hair-pinned left onto Pescadores and shifted down to second for an arduous climb into the hills. Thick stands of bamboo and palms of rain forest density blotted out sun and sky, dropping the temperature beneath the black-green canopy of foliage to the point where I actually got goosebumps on my arms.

I climbed at a steady twenty-degree angle for some several minutes, passing an occasional peasant lugging baskets of fruit, fish, vegetables, or dry goods uphill on rounded back or the swayed spines of burros. Then the pitch of my engine whined down as the Skyhawk topped a rise and proceeded on a gentle grade along an unpaved road just wide enough to accommodate two passing cars if their paint jobs weren't too thick. Here I encountered the first in a row of handsome stucco villas, some cantilevered precariously over ledges above the sea, others set shyly back behind heavy stone or iron gates strangled with thick vines resplendent with bright berries, hibiscus, bougainvillea, orchids and wild roses, every kind of flower imaginable except the daisies for which Smiley Kruger's villa had been named. Which is why I almost missed it.

It was one of the more imposing estates, occupying a couple of acres sharply demarcated by a four-foot-high stone wall topped by forbidding spearpoints, and a double gate of bars as thick as those of a prison. The house was pink sandstone and a darker stucco surrounded by a veranda. In the sweeping driveway, a Lincoln Continental gleamed ominous black, its sheen being brought to perfection by a chauffeur in shirt sleeves. A withered gardener poked lethargically at a flower border around the house, and a brindle boxer, panting but alert, guarded the veranda. I stopped before the gate for a moment to take in the layout but moved on when the chauffeur looked at me over his shoulder.

I hadn't determined until then what I was going to do—take my balls in hand and walk brazenly up to the gate demanding to see Señor Kruger, or play it a little cooler and observe the activity around the estate until I got a clearer reading of the layout and its possible defenses. I opted for the latter, though it would take longer. Much longer I didn't have. It was late Friday afternoon. The time I had to determine if Jimmy was on the premises, to find him and get him home, could be reckoned no longer in days, but in hours. Still, sniffing around Las Margaritas seemed more desirable than coming on like Cher Bond. With the beautiful thing Smiley Kruger had going for him down here, any threat to his tranquility might be greeted with something substantially less than appreciation.

Typically, I was unarmed, partly by choice, partly by inertia. I can handle a gun just fine, having been a combat instructor during my hitch in the army. But I'm loath to carry a weapon, first of all, because weapons beget weapons and the mere showing of a piece can provoke gunplay that can be avoided if you confront your antagonist empty-handed. Second, weapons go off, and the notion of shooting someone is only a little less repulsive to me than the notion of being shot. And third—and here's where inertia comes in—I somehow never really expect things to come to gunplay. In my normal line of work, an irreconcilable dispute is settled by lawsuit at the very worst. It's only when my line of work becomes abnormal that the need for something more potent than my wits or my tongue manifests itself, by which time it's frequently too late. I guess deep down I believe everybody's as good-natured as myself and it always comes as a bit of a shock to me when things get so nasty you have to resort to weapons.

I wonder what my Indian-fighting ancestors would do if they heard me talking this way!

Anyway, at this moment I didn't have the wherewithal to swat a mosquito so it behooved me to proceed a little cautiously. I drove a hundred yards or so beyond the villa, into a kind of miniature marketplace occupied by a handful of roadside vendors hawking junk jewelry and embroidered hats and serapes to gringo tourists descending from the central plateau to the coastal resorts. That gave me an idea. I haggled for a straw hat and a serape, donned them, and walked back down the road to Las Margaritas. There I hunkered down in front of the gate, looking a little, I trust, like a mestizo resting from a trek out of the mountains.

Fifteen minutes of this posturing netted me nothing more than admiration for the peons who could maintain this position for hours at a time. Then I lucked out as Smiley Kruger stepped out on the veranda for a moment, said something to his chauffeur and returned through the front screen door. I'd never met Kruger but I'd seen pictures of him, a tall, barrel-chested man with a bald head fringed with dark blond hair. He was dressed in white cord slacks and a pastel blue polo shirt with an emblem over the left breast and white shoes. He'd carried a tall drink with him and gestured with it as he instructed his chauffeur. He radiated an air of command and from the way the chauffeur, gardener, and even the boxer had kind of snapped to in that brief moment, I got a sense of his conducting his estate with more military authority than domestic. These men were probably armed and the dog trained to do disagreeable things to people's wrists and ankles.

I'd hoped that whatever Kruger said to the chauffeur was an indication that he would soon be leaving the estate but this turned out to be wishful thinking and half an hour later, I was still asquat, watching an uncommonly boring tableau of hired hands doing their jobs.

I didn't know whether to go or stay or attempt to penetrate. I reassessed the last option and wondered if, with a little doctoring of my clothes, I could gain entry to the estate posing as a peasant. My Spanish is excellent, having been brought up by Mexican servants, I can even capture the subtleties of Mexican accents and idioms. But whether my command of the tongue was good enough to fool Kruger's Mexican help was debatable. My winter-pale complexion wouldn't help, either. I often wish I was a larger-than-life hero but when you're standing unarmed before a houseful of potential cutthroats contemplating fooling them with a disguise, you may well as I did opt to remain a smaller-than-life chicken-shit. And so I squatted outside mulling the situation over and wondering how long I could maintain this posture before my joints locked into a permanent fetal position.

What ultimately made up my mind was the very rain-squall I'd predicted. I could feel the wind shift as if it had bumped into a brick wall and bounced off in the opposite direction, seaward. Ferocious black clouds roiled over the hills and dipped into the slope on which these estates lay, angry foggy fingers snatching at the tall trees and twanging them like fork tines. I looked around for cover. A number of peasants, who'd been hunkered down themselves, didn't bother to move. They knew, with that timeless resignation of the mestizo, that after they got drenched, the sun would come out and dry them up again, or maybe it wouldn't and they'd catch their death of cold and die. So they just sat there like stones as the first blast of icy rain struck us like the dousing of a waterfall.

Me, I'm not big on timeless resignation. In fact, I said to myself, "Fuck this shit!" and whippity-assed back to my car. I sat there for fifteen minutes until the storm subsided, the sun reappeared, and the patter of raindrops through the tiers of foliage dwindled to a whisper. I got out of my car, sunned myself till my damp clothes were warm and crisp like fresh laundry, then climbed into the car and waited some more. Somehow I fell asleep, for the next thing I remembered, it was dusky, the rim of the orange sun pulling magnificent ribbons of blue and pink clouds with it into the western horizon. A moment later the gates of Las Margaritas opened and Kruger's Continental nosed out, turning left into the camino and descending toward the coast road. I couldn't make out whether Kruger was in the car and I had to make a quick decision as to whether I should follow or stay behind and try gaining entry to his villa.

I started my car, turned around, and rolled downhill until I was in front of the gates which the gardener had just closed. He was trudging back to the villa, trailed by the dog. On the veranda, a grubby Mexican stood in soiled white linens and huaraches, holding an ancient but presumably serviceable carbine. That put the lid on my notion of sneaking into Las

Margaritas. I accelerated and followed the dust trail of Kruger's car, catching sight of it just as it reached the foot of the hill and veered left, south toward Acapulco.

If you're going to tail somebody, you really should do it on the Pacific coast road south of Manzanillo at sunset. You may lose sight of your mark and maybe drive off a precipice and into the treacherous rocks far below but as an esthetic experience, it's hard to beat. At times, the highway dips close to sea level, filling the car with the aroma of salt and seaweed, then it rolls up into dark hills and through tunnels of vegetation whose tendrils swipe at your car like hungry living things. We passed through a number of tiny resort towns along this stretch of the Mexican Riviera, then rose into the hills one last time before plunging down into Acapulco, past Las Brisas, one of the great resort hotels in all the world, and into the Miami Beach-like strip of brightly lit hotels that bordered the graceful sweep of shoreline from Morning Beach to Afternoon Beach.

The Continental snaked past this strip, continuing south into the native quarter, a tightly packed semi-slum that sweltered even after the sun had gone down. Decaying row houses and stores that were scarcely more than concession stands huddled together in squalor and Mexican music mingled with American rock blared over storefront loudspeakers while lottery vendors touted lucky numbers into the purple darkness.

At length, we pulled up to a large, hangar-like building of brown concrete and adobe out of which large chunks had crumbled and fallen away to expose the naked stone beneath. I recognized the jai-alai frontón at once and spliced my Skyhawk into the line of automobiles inching into a parking lot. I followed the Continental past a wildly gesticulating parking attendant and took a space two or three cars beyond it, then peered into the black night to see who got out of the car.

It was Kruger.

I got out and followed him and his chauffeur-bodyguard into the frontón, bought my ticket, and breasted my way through crowds of spectators and up into the stands where Kruger was selecting a seat. Kruger was wearing the same pastel clothes he'd worn earlier but had taken off his dark glasses. His chauffeur was a slight man in a powder-blue uniform and cap and that bulge over his heart was either a shoulder-holstered gun or the beginnings of a rudimentary left breast. He searched for faces, friendly, unfriendly, familiar and unfamiliar, sweeping a full 360 degrees before lowering himself into a wooden seat beside his boss. Every time someone came up the aisle and took a seat in their vicinity, this weasel-looking dude would study him.

His dark eyes fixed on me as I climbed the stairs, looking aimlessly about as if the selection of a seat was a matter of complete indifference to me. He twisted in his chair as I settled into a seat directly behind him on the aisle and studied me with a directness that would have embarrassed a hypnotist. I willed myself to look like a typical American tourist, rubbernecking at the three-wall court screened off from spectators as if I'd never seen a frontón before.

Actually, I'd seen quite a bit of jai-alai in Mexico as well as in Miami and Tampa. In 1968, I'd seen the spectacular Mirapeix brothers of Spain, Eduardo and José, in a fantastic match with France, and been hooked ever since. There was some good amateur jai-alai played in Florida, not a little of it by Americans like Bob Grossberg and Fred Petit, Randy Lazenby and Ken Burris, Joe Cornblit and Charles Nickerson. The pro movement was picking up momentum, and the sport was moving out of Florida—three frontóns had gone up in Connecticut. I'd quietly made a note to explore representation with some pros if the sport ever really took hold in the United States. Why it hasn't, I've never been sure, since it's probably the fastest and most challenging sport in the world. Even the best-conditioned athletes are burnt-out cases by their mid-twenties.

A doubles preliminary was already under way with the Blue team, listed on my card as Miguel Gomez and José Melindez, battling the Red team; Juan Camagüey and Vicente García in a rather lethargic contest that was still three times faster than a tennis match could ever hope to be. The players, in slacks and polo shirts, sneakers and helmets (which many players disdained to wear), collected the concrete-hard, goatskin-encased pelota on its 150-mph rebound from one of the three walls in their gracefully curved wicker cestas and rocketed it back against the front wall with a lithe motion that was pure ballet.

In front of me, Kruger and his bodyguard studied their programs, glancing up occasionally when there was a gasp from the crowd or a whistled expression of displeasure. Up and down the aisles, white-clad Mexican touts carrying trays of tennis balls hawked their services in what for me is the unique aspect of the game, and one almost as exciting as the play itself—the betting.

Like horse- and dog-racing, betting is done at parimutuel windows with the usual range of wagers offered at various denominations. You can bet win, place, and show on the various teams that will face each other in round-robin competition on one evening's card. There are also the complicated combinations like exacta, perfecta, and Daily Double. But that's where the resemblance ends because in jai-alai, as the score changes in the course of the match, the odds change and you're permitted to make a bet with these roving touts at the new odds. It's like betting on a horserace after each furlong. For instance, suppose the Red team is a favorite. It may go off at, say, 3—2 odds when the match begins. And suppose it wins the first five points. Then the odds of Red winning may stretch to 10-to-1. If you fanatically believe in Blue, you'll take the odds in the hope of winning ten pesos for every one you wager. Now, suppose Blue has a fantastic streak and wins eight or nine points in a row, to lead Red 9—5. The odds may now shift in Blue's favor to something like 2-to-1. Now, what does the Blue bettor do? He picks Red to win. Why? Because he is now certain of winning money. If Blue wins, the bettor wins money at 10-to-1 odds. If Blue loses, the bettor wins money at 2-to-1 odds. By hedging his bets, shrewdly playing the odds, and balancing the amounts of money you wager, you can come out winning no matter what you do. Needless to say, you can also come out losing.

The touts carry old tennis balls slit partially open to accommodate a betting slip. The spectators call out to the tout after each point. He throws them these balls and the bettors write their bets on the slips and throw the balls with the slips in them back to him. He pockets the slips, turns to watch the next point, then barks out the new odds.

At the height of a closely contested game, the air is filled with the shouts of touts advertising the new odds, bettors bidding for the touts' attention, the screams and cheers of spectators, and tennis balls. The place becomes an absolute madhouse and how these touts manage to keep track of the score, the odds, their senses, and their balance on the steep aisle stairs is a miracle which could give the Virgin of Guadalupe a good run for the money.

But these touts plying their way up and down the stands suggested the solution to my problem of separating Kruger from his bodyguard and I sat back to watch the matches waiting for an opportunity.

Red won the first match and thus the right to face the next team in the round-robin, a handsome couple of kids from Zihuatanejo named Joaquin and Langustana, who now assumed the Blue color and took up the challenge. Kruger, who'd been almost completely indifferent to the results of the first match, placed a bet on this one, as did his compañero, as well as yours truly. Now the two of them leaned forward to watch the action.

Jai-alai is a handball game in which, instead of striking the ball with the palm of your hand, you have to catch it in a long curved basket and hurl it in one continuous motion against a granite wall (no other natural substance could take the pounding). Your opponent has to pick it up in his basket on no more than one bounce as it comes off the front wall, or off the side wall known as the ble, or off the back wall called the rebote.

Now, the thing is, you have to decide where the ball is going to bounce, what kind of spin it's going to have, and how you're going to play it in a little less than two seconds because in the time it takes you to say "Jesus, here it comes!" that pelota will have traveled some 220 feet. I once put a cesta on and walked out on a frontón just to see what it was like. I stayed for one point, during which time my consuming concern was what would happen if that mother hit me in a vital or even non-vital organ.

So you can imagine what it takes not merely to catch the pelota in your cesta but to do it gracefully and sometimes acrobatically. These guys do on every shot what Al Gionfriddo did once against the Yankees in the World Series.

With one eye on the pair in front of me, I watched the Reds and Blues performing incredible rebotes off the back walls, chulas, bote prontos, and chic chacs that defy description. As the score climbed, the excitement in the auditorium swelled and the din became almost painful. Both

Kruger and his bodyguard began calling for tennis balls to slip their bets into and as the score teetered, Kruger hedged his bets several times. The final points were coming up and the spectators were almost crazed with betting lust. At that moment, two touts were working back to back in the aisle next to me. This was the moment. With my right hand, I shoved one into another, with my left I rabbit-chopped the chauffeur at the base of his neck. His reflexes stiffened him to his feet and I pushed him into the aisle.

In that one instant, there were more tennis balls in the air than you can find over the courts of the West Side Tennis Club on a busy night. Spectators within a twenty-foot range were showered with them. The commotion and confusion were unimaginable as the touts tried to collect the balls, spectators scurried after them, everyone lost track of the game, and several burly police descended on the chauffeur, thinking he'd somehow started the ruckus.

While the aisle swarmed like a disturbed ants' nest, I produced out of my jacket a Coke bottle I'd nicked from the concession stand while I was up at the windows making my bet on the second match. From the feverish gambling I've just described, anyone who knows Mexicans knows why bringing Coke bottles to your seat is strictly prohibido. I jammed the mouth of my bottle against Kruger's right ear and said, "Kruger, this is .32-caliber revolver. How would you like me to perform a chula on your head?" A chula is a jai-alai shot translatable as "killer."

He tried to look over his shoulder, but I jammed him harder. "Who are you? What do you want?"

"Slide out of the aisle to your left," I commanded. "Do anything dumb and I'll wax the frontón floor with your brains."

He rose out of his seat and began stepping over spectators, moving away from what was now a near riot in the aisles whose focal point was the inert body of the unconscious chauffeur.

He stepped into the aisle and proceeded down the stairs and through the tunnel with me pressing close behind him, my Coke bottle in my jacket pocket. We walked briskly past guards at the turnstiles and out into the warm, damp evening. In the dim light of the parking lot, Kruger pivoted to get a look at my face. I smacked him in the mouth with the bottle and hustled him against a parked car, frisking him nimbly while he reeled rubber-legged over the hood. I found a .25-caliber automatic strapped to his right leg. I substituted it for my Coke bottle and suddenly felt a lot more secure about things.

"Fachrissake, will you tell me what this is all about?" he whined as blood dripped out of his mouth and puddled on the hood of the car. I spun him around. He looked into my eyes, fearful, confused.

"Kruger, I came for Jimmy Quinn."

"Jimmy Quinn? Mister, I don't know what you're—"

I lifted my foot and stamped on his instep with my boot, which really smarts. He bellowed and started limping around in a tight circle, cursing. "That's the wrong answer, Kruger," I said, following him with my gun like a lion trainer in a circus ring.

Kruger hobbled over to the car and leaned on it, rubbing his foot and panting. He looked at me and pleaded, "At least tell me who you are, why you want Quinn."

"I'm Dave Bolt, his agent."

"Oh, so you're Dave Bolt!"

"You sound almost glad."

"I am glad. Yeah, I've got Jimmy."

"In what condition? Because if it's anything less than mint, I'm gonna use your balls for barracuda bait out there in Acapulco Bay."

"He's all right. I had to punch him out a little to tame him, but he's all right. You'd be doing me a great favor by taking him off my hands. Your car or mine?"

"Mine'll do. It's over there," I said, motioning with the gun.

Distrustful, I walked behind him, training the muzzle of his .25 on the small of his back. I decided to let him drive; it would be easier to cover him. I opened the driver's-side door for him then hustled around to the passenger's side and got in. "Drive with care, Kruger. The life you save may be your own." I handed him the keys.

He started the car and we cruised out of the parking lot. "You played for the Dallas Cowboys, right?" he said amiably, as if we were neighbors commuting to work. "I think I remember you. I doubt if you remember me, though. While you glamour boys were running your pass patterns, I was knocking my helmet off in the pit. You got injured, right? Larry Wilson took you out, if I'm not mistaken. . . Yeah, that was a shame. You had a lot of talent I even remember once, you—"

"Stow the small talk, Kruger. What's with Jimmy?"

"He's okay, I told you." Kruger's voice was nasal, the product of a nose pulped times without reckoning in his days as a Baltimore Colt lineman. "I've got him in a cottage on the grounds of my villa. He's under guard and believe me when I tell you I'd like nothing more than to let him go. He's just one big fuckin' nuisance, that guy."

"What's stopping you?" We were now cruising past the first of the hotels.

"He won't go! He refuses to leave until I pay him back the money he invested with me. You know about that, the money he invested with me?"

"Is that what you call it? An investment?"

He looked at me. In the streetlights along the broad avenue that skirted the beach, the congealed blood on his chin and lower lip took on a gruesome purple hue. "Bolt, I never guaranteed a return on his money or anybody else's. You invest with me, you're risking your capital, same as if you invest with a Merrill, Lynch broker."

"Cut the horseshit, Kruger. You sucked those guys in—to say nothing of the Dolores Pleasances you had in God knows how many cities—with increasing returns on their small investments. Then when you'd captured their trust, you kicked the point out from under the pyramid and skipped down here with a small fortune. Jimmy's followed you down here to get his money back and the money his friends entrusted with him."

Kruger gave a monumental shrug. "I don't have it, Bolt! I lost it on this Australian investment. The deal fell through, this development syndicate pulled out and now the land is worth zilch. Hell, I offered Jimmy a dollar an acre, which is something, but he wants a full refund and he won't budge till he gets it."

I studied Kruger out of the corner of my eye. Sincerity was written all over his features but he was lying to beat the band. It was easy to see how smoothly he'd taken in Jimmy and Dolores Pleasance and all the other suckers, for he radiated honesty and there was no way to prove or disprove anything he said. It was clear to me he was running a variation of the pyramid con but though it tasted like poison to admit it, there was nothing I could do except take Jimmy home with me, empty-handed.

Kruger, mainly out of nervousness, talked football during the hour or so it took us to drive up the western flank of Mexico to Manzanillo. He knew everything and everybody in the game and dropped Johnny Unitases and O. J. Simpsons and Calvin Hills and Bob Grieses into his conversation as easily as a man salts his food. His patter was engaging, the skilled rap of an accomplished bunco artist. I had no doubt that after lying low for a while after this debacle, he'd surface again to ply his flim-flam somewhere else around the National Football League, coming on convincingly as an ex-jock who'd lucked into a good thing and wanted nothing more than to share it with his dear friends in this wonderful American sport of football. And though I think most football players are honest or can be kept honest by present-day rules and intensive supervision, few of them are exempt from the law of human nature that says there's a little bit of larcenist in all of us.

It was almost midnight when we turned up Camino de los Pescadores and climbed the winding, bumpy road to Kruger's estate. Kruger got out and pushed the button of a bell beside the gate and after a minute, a servant stumbled down the steps of the villa trailed by the snarling dog and opened the huge iron gate for us. I made Kruger get back in the car with me and we drove up to the front door. I was inclined to believe his story about Jimmy being held captive on the premises and refusing to leave but as this man lied as facilely and compulsively as a Southern politician, I kept the little pistol trained on him.

He shut off the engine and we stepped into the night, an incredibly bright, star-filled evening redolent with the perfume of a million exotic flowers and salt air and alive with the chirps of crickets, toads, night birds, and an occasional nocturnal beast yowling in lust or hunger or defiance.

Kruger led me along a slate path around the side of his villa, across a broad tiled patio with ghostly white metal lawn furniture glistening with night dew, through a vined arboretum reeking of jasmine and gardenia, and up to the door of one of half a dozen cabin-sized guest cottages arrayed in a semicircle around a lighted fountain.

"Some beautiful setup, huh, Dave?" Kruger, addressing me with easy familiarity, warbled. "Listen, any time you want to come down here, you let me know, I'll put you up. Bring your girl or leave that department to me. Tell me what your taste is, I'll have her waiting in your bed when you arrive."

"I'm much obliged," I said, peering through the bright print curtain over the picture window of the cottage and trying to make out the form that seemed to flit from one side of the room to another as Kruger shook out a key chain looking for the right key.

My grip on the gun tensed as he pressed his biceps to the door and stepped into a beautifully decorated hideaway, florid printed fabrics, expensive imported Italian furniture, excellent works of Mexican art gracing the walls. Though I'd seen someone in here through the curtain on the picture window, it seemed deserted. "Dominguez, you here?" Kruger called in Spanish, stepping into the living room tentatively.

He paused, suddenly cautious. Something was wrong. He looked over his shoulder at me and I gestured with my head for him to step farther into the room. He took two steps and stopped again as he saw what I saw at the same moment. The inert body of a man crumpled on the floor beside a large mahogany breakfront. I glimpsed his jet hair and knew at once, with some relief, that this wasn't Jimmy.

It took me only a fraction of a second to realize that Jimmy had somehow overpowered his guard and was still in the cottage but before I could act on my realization, Jimmy's arm thrust out of a service bay in the wall between living room and kitchen. In his hand was a brutal-looking long-barreled pistol that looked more like a portable siege weapon than a sidearm. "Stop right there, motherfucker," Jimmy ordered.

Kruger froze as if he'd just been cast in bronze. Through clenched teeth he said, "Watch out with that thing, will ya, Jimmy? It leaves enormous holes in people."

"I know. I'm planning to leave one in you," Jimmy said.

"Put it down, for Christ's sake. I'm already captured, can't you see?"

Jimmy couldn't see. I was out of his range. "By who?"

"By me, Jimmy. Dave," I said. "I've got the man covered. Come on out."

The weapon withdrew and a moment later Jimmy rounded the bend of the kitchen. He looked none the worse for his ordeal except that Kruger had outfitted him in resort clothes a size too big and he had a two-day stubble of blond prickles on his cheeks. He was a big, strapping boy with a veritable hayrick of straw-colored hair and crystal blue eyes that must have broken a million hearts.

He lowered his gun and grinned at me. "Dave! How'd you find me?"

"It was easy. You're the only quarterback in professional football who's been missing all week."

He chuckled, then gestured in the direction of the unconscious Dominguez. "You should have told your man I have the best completion record in the Central Division," he said to Kruger. "He turned his back on me for just a second and I hit him on the head with an ashtray from here to there. Play went for ten yards and a first down. My first down, Kruger. I control the game now and I want my money." He had raised his gun again and was pointing it at Kruger's midsection. Unconsciously I stepped to one side, not trusting Kruger's body, muscular and substantial though it was, to stop a slug from the blunderbuss Jimmy had copped from Dominguez. Kruger looked over his shoulder at me, silently requesting my intercession.

"What're you looking at him for?" Jimmy asked Kruger. "He's on my team."

"Say something to him, will ya, Bolt? The kid's hand is shaking; he's likely to blow me away by accident."

Jimmy suddenly became uptight as he realized there was some ambiguity in my feelings. He sidled to his left, once again putting Kruger between us as a buffer. I did of course have a gun in my hand and Jimmy didn't know now where my loyalties lay in view of Kruger's plea for me to reason with Jimmy. "Dave? You have something to say to me?"

"Yes, but I'm not sure this Mexican standoff with our friend Kruger in the middle is the perfect environment for a calm conversation. Why don't we sit down and talk?"

"Not until you put the gun away, Dave. I'm not sure if I should trust you. I thought you came down here to help me get my money back from this cocksucker. Apparently, you have something else in mind."

"I came to bring you back to the United States. You have a game on Sunday, and if you miss it, you're gonna bring more harm raining down than Samson ever dreamed of."

"I don't give a shit. I'm not leaving here until this crook gives me back every penny he stole from me and my friends."

"Jimmy," Kruger protested with a tired whimper, "I keep telling you—"

"Don't say it," Jimmy hissed, brandishing the gun wildly. "I don't want to hear that jive again. I just want my money."

Kruger shifted unconsciously to one side as if it would put him out of the line of fire but Jimmy and I shifted with him, circling slightly in a kind of deadly minuet around a human maypole.

"Jimmy," I said, "there's no way you can prove Kruger hoodwinked you. You take your money from him at gunpoint, he'll report it as robbery."

"He doesn't give me his money at gunpoint, this gunpoint's gonna make a loud noise."

"Don't be a jerk," I pleaded. "Look, at this moment you're in trouble but if you come home with me right away, I can square it for you. But if you persist in this grandstand play, you'll not only be ruined, you'll be thrown in prison. Think about that, Jim. The turn of the twenty-first century is less than twenty-five years away. You might be behind bars to greet it."

Jimmy's gun wavered, then firmed. "Some agent you are. I suppose this is your idea of standing up for your clients!"

"I stood up for you when I told you to check with me before investing your money in shady schemes. You ignored my advice. Consider yourself lucky I still care enough about you to risk my neck chasing you around the North American continent."

He blinked several times in rapid succession and I could tell he was debating with himself. I'd scored some telling points but I could see that nothing I'd said was sufficient to push him over the brink. I had one more argument left and if that didn't work there'd probably be bloodshed. Whose blood would be shed, I didn't know but the prospect that mine might be stimulated me to put every ounce of sincerity I possessed into my final plea.

"He's offered you a settlement, Jim."

"Sure. At twenty-five cents on the dollar. What am I supposed to tell my friends when I face them?"

"Tell them the truth," I said. "Tell them they're as stupid as you are."

Kruger actually twitched like a corpse jolted by an electric shock. "C'mon, Dave, that kind of remark isn't calculated to extend my life expectations. Cool it, huh?" he begged.

Jimmy was breathing heavily but his anger had been diverted from Kruger and was now directed at me, though in truth it was directed at himself. Here's where I played my trump card. "I know a way for you to recover every penny you lost."

His eyelids narrowed, partially smothering the fire in his eyes.

"What's that?"

"I'll tell you on the plane."

"This is a trick."

"No trick. In fact, I'll back it with my own money, that's a solemn pledge."

He stared into my eyes and read candor in them. Then he shook his head. "I don't want your money, I want his." He waved his gun insanely at Kruger but it was really the last spasm of a man who'd already made up his mind. Kruger ducked and feinted comically. Apparently, Kruger wasn't convinced Jimmy had made up his mind, because he threw up his hands in a gesture of surrender.

"All right, all right, I'll give you back half but that's my final offer."

Jimmy looked past him at me. I was nodding so rapidly I looked like I'd come down with Parkinson's disease. If he didn't take the money and run, he was an even bigger fool than I'd thought. "Okay," he said. "But I want it tonight, in cash."

"Sure, sure, no problem, no problem," Kruger stammered, collapsing in an armchair. I got a look at his face for the first time since we'd entered the cottage. It was beaded with sweat and his shirt was saturated from neck to belly.

"While you're at it," I added, "throw in another five thousand for Dolores Pleasance."

"Dolores—!" He almost levitated out of the chair. "That's how you traced me. That cunt!"

"To hear her tell it, she was your one-and-only. How fickle men are—after they've bilked gay divorcées out of their savings."

"I'll find a way to get even with you, Bolt."

"Submit it in triplicate. I'll take it under advisement. Meanwhile, there's one more thing."

"Christ, now what?"

"I want you to write out a statement saying that Jimmy has been a guest of yours since Monday, enjoying the hospitality while recovering from a strained shoulder."

"That's all?"

"That's all. But hear me out, Kruger. If I ever learn you've been talking to any member of the National Football League, I'll kick your ass from here to Chapultepec."

"Don't worry," he said. But then, what else could he say? He and I both knew perfectly well he'd be back in business two hours after I left him.

"Now, what's the first plane out of Manzanillo tomorrow morning?" I asked.

Kruger went to a liquor caddie and poured himself a brimming six-ounce glass of Scotch. "I don't know but it can't leave early enough to suit me."

He quaffed half the glass and gestured at the door. We glanced back at Dominguez, who still lay exactly as we'd found him, snoring; he'd present no problem for the nonce. We left the cottage and followed Kruger back to his villa but before reaching the main house he veered left and led us to a row of squat cabañas flanking the south side of his swimming pool. One of them was heavily padlocked. He reached into his pocket and produced a set of keys and opened the padlock, tossing it on the ground. He opened the door and flipped on a light.

It was a tight little room, furnished with a chair and table, a chest of drawers, and a wooden wardrobe. He looked over his shoulder at us regretfully, then pulled the wardrobe away from the wall. Behind it was the door of a wall safe. Shielding the dial from our eyes with his body, he twisted the dial several times until there was a metallic click, then pushed down on a heavy handle. The door swung open with a raspy noise, and he started to reach in. "That'll be fine, Kruger," I said, jamming my gun between his shoulder blades. Lucky I did. Wedged among several stacks of American and Mexican currency and legal papers was a .32 automatic.

He stepped away and looked at me. "Just take the gun, huh? Let me count out the money."

I stepped in front of him and pulled the gun out by the handle, removed the clip and pocketed it, and threw the gun on the floor. I paused to gaze at the stacks of cash: there must have been close to a million dollars in there. I whistled. "You don't believe in banks, do you?"

"You know your Mexican history, do you?" he asked. "It's safer to put your money in a paper shredder." He reached for a stack of greenbacks and began thumbing through it. I looked at Jimmy. The sight of all that dough had made his eyes bulge and I knew what was going through his mind. "Forget it, Jimmy. We made a bargain," I said.

Jimmy's hand trembled over the cannon he'd stuffed into the waistband of his trousers and I made ready to pounce. "All that money," he muttered.

"Remember," I reminded him, "you started with a thousand and you ended up with twenty-five. The man is giving you back half—you're still ahead." I kept up this line of patter while Kruger riffled through the thick wad of bills, tossed it back in the safe and slammed the safe door shut, spinning the dial vigorously, before the sight of all that money could make Jimmy renege on his bargain. Kruger handed Jimmy a tidy pile of hundred-dollar bills. The kid counted them out while I covered Kruger, whose burnished face had, not surprisingly, acquired a sickly pallor. "There should be sixty thousand there," I said. "Half of your group's investment, plus five thousand for Dolores Pleasance." It took about ten minutes to complete the count-out, at the end of which Jimmy nodded. I then made Kruger write out that note confirming Jimmy had spent the last few days as his guest down here. I pocketed it snugly in my jacket, it was Jimmy's ticket to credibility, and I didn't want anything to happen to it.

We stuffed the money into a beach bag and returned to the car, holding Kruger hostage until we'd started the car and the gates were open. I emitted a big sigh of relief as we turned into Pescadores.

It was premature.

Just as we'd begun the descent to the coastal highway, a pair of bright headlights pierced the thick foliage ahead of us. A car was rounding the last curve before the villa, and from the high whine of its engine, it was coming fast.

A second later the shafts of light straightened out and impaled us. It could be anyone but I suspected it was someone in particular. We slowed to a crawl to pass each other and the make of the car resolved itself in my own headlights. It was Kruger's Lincoln Continental. I locked eyes with the chauffeur as I passed abeam of him. Was it my imagination or was he highly displeased to see me?

The moment I'd cleared, I kicked the throttle. In five seconds, he'd reach the gate of Las Margaritas where Kruger would raise the hue and cry and send him back down after us. I didn't hear the hue and cry above the roar of our engine and the scrabble of stones kicking the chassis over my spinning wheels but a glance in the mirror soon revealed headlights and I congratulated myself on my choice of rented car. A gaily painted Volkswagen is at a distinct handicap against a Lincoln Continental. I wondered if even my Buick would fare much better.

"Here they come," Jimmy said twisting around in the front seat. I glanced at the mirror and reckoned I had about a thousand-yard advantage. We reached the coast road and I swung right and floored the accelerator. We lurched forward with a screech and zoomed toward Manzanillo. A moment later I heard the echo of the Lincoln's tires and the chase was on. We flashed through Manzanillo as quickly as if it were the grandstand of a stock-car racecourse. A few instants later the fork loomed up where the road diverged, one branch to the airport, the other to the resort town of Las Hadas. My impulse was to head for the airport but I overruled it. I didn't know the road very well, whereas Kruger's chauffeur would know every inch of it. Even if he didn't overtake us, what would we do when we got there? Shoot it out? It was too late to catch a plane, anyway, the last one for Mexico City had departed hours ago.

I veered left and kicked the car into overdrive. Ahead of us, the ghostly white minarets of the Las Hadas complex shimmered like a fairy castle in a Walt Disney movie. Jimmy twitched. "What are you doing, man? They don't allow cars in this area!"

"I know. That's what I'm counting on." We whipped through the imposing portals at sixty miles an hour past a uniformed guard whose eyes widened to the size of dinner plates. He was so astonished he could only raise his hand feebly in a futile gesture to halt us. But I knew he'd be prepared for Kruger's car. Jimmy confirmed it.

"He's stopping the Lincoln!"

"Good. Now hang on."

Luckily, the sweeping driveway up to the hotel was almost devoid of pedestrians at this late hour and I was able to negotiate the circle and head back for the portal without much loss of speed. A couple of honeymooners strolling in the moonlight gaped with disbelief as we whipped past them, shattering the night quiet with the scream of our tires. I stood on the gas pedal as we approached the exit side of the guard's house and glimpsed the guard gesticulating wildly at the chauffeur. Beside him, I could make out Kruger's apoplectic face and flailing hands as he watched us hurtle past. I didn't know how long the guard could detain him but it might be long enough for us to give him the slip.

I gunned back down the coast road and punched the headlight switch, plunging us into darkness. It seemed like a clever idea because once Kruger disengaged from the guard, he'd have no taillights to follow and would have to guess which road we'd taken. Knowing we wanted to get to the airport, he might choose that road, which is why I ignored it at the fork and continued down the coast road to Acapulco. The problem, of course, was that while Kruger couldn't see me, I couldn't see the road. Save for the shimmer of a quarter moon and the stars, all partially obscured by a haze, I had nothing to illuminate a road which is treacherous even in bright daylight driving at normal speed. I slowed to a cautious crawl, looking in the mirror. Headlights blinded me momentarily—Kruger's chauffeur was quit of the guard. And he'd plunged past the fork in the road without a moment's indecision. I clapped my forehead as I realized I'd given us away; by hitting the brake, I'd flashed my brake lights at the pursuing car. I might as well have set off a red flare. Dumb, Bolt. Very dumb.

I flipped the headlights on again and gunned on down the coast road. Not only had I blown a chance to make a clean getaway, I'd lost half my lead. The road twisted along the coastline as if it had been laid out by an engineer stoned on peyote. The Buick had more maneuverability than its pursuer but Kruger's chauffeur obviously knew the road intimately and gained on us. "What do you think A. J. Foyt would do under these circumstances?" I asked Jimmy.

"Same as you're doing—hope for a miracle. Do you think if I shot at them. . .? It works in the movies."

"Yeah, but in the movies people usually shoot back. But if you could plug their radiator. . ."

"Plug it? A direct hit with this thing," he said, taking Dominguez's siege weapon out of the waistband of his pants, "and I could reduce that car to scrap metal. But the way this road weaves. . ."

He rolled down his window and leaned out, leveling his gun with his right hand while steadying his elbow with his left. "Think you can hit a stationary target?" I asked.

"Sure. What're you gonna do?"

"This." I hit my brake pedal. The nose of the car dipped as the speedometer needle dropped from seventy to fifteen in moments. It took the chauffeur a couple of seconds to react by which time he was less than a hundred yards away from us. His brakes squealed something awful and the Continental skittered precipitously close to the shoulder of the road, beyond which was a rockbound palisade and a long tumble into the sea. They screeched up within twenty-five yards of us and Jimmy opened fire. I think I'd have preferred to be standing next to an eighteen-inch naval gun. The explosion was terrific and Jimmy's hand jolted to the vertical. I thought I heard the clangor of metal but with my ears ringing, I don't think I could have made out the Dallas Symphony Orchestra if I'd been sitting in the brass section. Jimmy trained his gun and fired several more times. I craned my neck and saw a puff of steam curling out of the radiator of the Continental.

I grabbed Jimmy by the shirt and yanked him back into the car, pushing him down as I jumped on the accelerator. I hunched over the wheel just enough to see the road. I didn't hear their return fire but felt it as a slug clunked into the trunk. I shook the steering wheel violently and the car dipsy-doodled, giving them a poor target. A score on our gas tank and it was all over but it never came. A moment later, we rounded a hairpin turn, leaving their disabled car, and no doubt its owner and driver, steaming.

"You run a good zig-out pattern," Jimmy commented as I brought the car up to a sensible speed.

"Yeah, but now let's run a straight post for Acapulco."

Chapter XIV

• • • •

The following morning, I called NFL headquarters from Acapulco and was put through to Barry Posner in record time. "I've got Jimmy Quinn," I said.

I didn't expect a delirious response but at least Posner could have given me a little more satisfaction than "That's nice. Where are you?"

"Mexico. We'll be connecting with Braniff flight 758 out of Houston. We'll pull into Indianapolis at 4:32 Indianapolis time. Don't bother bringing flowers."

"I'll be there. We'll talk at the airport."

"You don't waste time."

"I don't, no."

"Can we call Jimmy's wife, at least?"

"No, not yet."

"What about the Racer brass?"

"I'll have them with me."

"What about the press?"

"Are you crazy?"

"No, I meant, can we keep them away?"

"What the hell do you take me for, Bolt?" He quickly realized he'd set himself up for a zinger and added, "Don't answer that. There'll be no press, unless Jimmy's recognized."

The hop from Acapulco was too short to catch any sleep but we managed to doze on the Houston flight and slumber deeply most of the way to Indianapolis. The plane was half filled and each of us was able to stretch across three seats. I awoke and looked at my watch. We were about half an hour out of Indianapolis. I crossed the aisle and nudged Jimmy. I hadn't had a chance to talk to him but I wanted him fully briefed and coached before we went into the meeting with Posner and the Racer people. We washed up but I denied Jimmy's request to shave. The reddish stubble on his face might help shield his identity from inquiring eyes at the airport.

We went over the story I'd fashioned for Jimmy and I interrogated him as critically as I knew Posner would do. Jimmy responded with a kind of innocent candor that was positively convincing. The story was not a particularly good one but it was the best I could come up with and I was counting on Jimmy's butter-wouldn't-melt-in-his-mouth ingenuousness to carry it. "If you hang cool in the pocket, you may squeeze out of this yet," I said and we went over it again.

I brooded for several minutes as the plane began its descent into Indianapolis. I had something else on my chest but getting it off was going to be exquisitely difficult and I assessed every phrase in my mind before permitting myself to broach it. "There's another thing I want to say to you," I finally said.

He tilted his head and looked at me openly.

"In the course of this brouhaha, I've had a number of talks with your wife." I said not even daring to call her by name. "This has been pretty rough on her."

"Hell, I'm sure it has," he said not yet seeing where I was leading him.

"She has no reason to stand by you, you know."

He ran a knuckle over the prickles on his cheek. "I'm not sure I follow you."

"She's told me all about your women," I elaborated.

"Ah. Yeah." He lapsed into an uneasy silence, fidgeting with the fabric on the arm of his seat. "There's never been anything serious, though. Just a lot of one-night stands, mainly, and those on the road for the most part. Jesus, Dave, these chicks all but beg to be balled. A man's got to be a saint."

"She's going to leave you, Jimmy."

"She told you that?"

"Uh-huh. Now, you can tell me it's none of my business but in a way it is, because with what she knows about this situation, she can blow your story wide open and ruin you. She has to have a good reason to back you up. You haven't given her one. Besides," I said, venturing into treacherous territory, "I can't imagine why you'd risk losing such a wonderful and devoted woman." Internally I winced at my own sententiousness but the only way I could convince him I had no personal interest in his wife was to come on like a Baptist preacher. "You also owe it to those kids," I said, laying on an extra portion of what Trish calls schmaltz.

I could feel my face reddening with embarrassment over this hypocritical performance and I had to avert my eyes to keep from exposing the guilt in them.

"You really think she's reached that point?" Jimmy said. "You really think she'd leave me?"

"She sounded sincere when she said it to me."

He put his hand on my arm, forcing me to look at him. His crystal eyes were glassy with incipient tears. "Thanks, Dave. Thanks for everything. You're a true friend."

Needless to say, at that moment I wanted to die.

I spotted Barry Posner at precisely the same moment that a man in the crowd at the gate spotted Jimmy Quinn.

I don't know who it was but I distinctly heard him say, "Isn't that Jimmy Quinn?" So much for Jimmy's beard. It was about as useful a disguise as a coat of paint on the World Trade Center.

"We've been made," I said to Posner locking steps with him as we hustled from the gate.

He muttered an oath. "You have any luggage?" he asked, leading us up a ramp.

"Yes, but it's still in my hotel room in Mexico, paying more rent in a day than I pay in a week. I'll retrieve it somehow. Where we going?"

He didn't bother answering but continued walking triple-time across the terminal floor. Put a sulky behind him and he'd have put in a respectable heat at Roosevelt Raceway. We passed through a complex of shops and concession stands, Jimmy striding with face buried in the collar of his shirt. I hoped the man who had spotted Jimmy would keep the news to himself but as the Indianapolis sports pages had been filled with little else besides speculation about his whereabouts, I didn't think that was much of a likelihood. Within minutes press people would pop up like bean sprouts in the terminal.

"There," said Posner, jaunting around a corner and gesturing at a door marked Airport Personnel Only. We stepped inside. It turned out to be a little lounge that had been cleared of airport habitués for this meeting. Pacing the room like a couple of sentries were Arthur Spartling and his coach Hobie Gilmore. Spartling looked even more harassed than the last time I'd seen him and possibly balder or grayer or both. A lot of Indianapolis hair had been lost or whitened in the past week and I reckon my own had not been unaffected. Hobie scowled and continued pacing. Neither of them bothered to offer a handshake or a word of welcome. The air was thick with trouble and anger. I made ready to lash myself to the mast for the coming storm.

Posner motioned for us to sit down in a couple of straight-backed chairs while he, Spartling, and Gilmore settled into comfortable seats facing us. He beamed rays of disapproval at us through his horn-rimmed glasses and fingered the knot of his silk tie, clearing his throat. He issued me a particularly nasty look and perverse as it sounds, I think he'd have liked nothing more than for me to fail in my mission of bringing Jimmy back just so he could have the satisfaction of see-ing me ruined. And my failure to bring Jimmy back might have been my ruination. Certainly, the existence of that list would have been brought out by continued investigation and even though that list represented nothing illegal—only imprudent—the questions it would have raised, coupled with Jimmy's disappearance and the betting irregularity last Monday and Al Negri's murder, would have smeared us both seriously and perhaps fatally.

But that list no longer existed. I'd burned it. From Mex-ico, I'd called Ladrue Retting and told him to call the rest of the Suicide Squad and tell them to keep their mouths shut. All stories were squared. I'd coached Jimmy to a fare-thee-well and he sat beside me as cool as a Coors on a summer day. We had a chance of beating this rap.

Posner stared at me. "I don't suppose you'd like to wait outside while we talk to Jimmy privately," he opened.

"Sorry, it won't do you any good. I've instructed him not to say boo to you unless I'm in the same room—myself, or an attorney. If you'd prefer an attorney, of course. . ."

He sighed. "All right, all right." He turned to Jimmy and plunged into the questioning with the delicacy of a bowling ball. "Now, Quinn, where've you been since Monday night?"

Jimmy cleared his throat. "Manzanillo, Mexico."

"Doing what?"

"Taking care of some personal business."

"Be specific."

"I was looking into an investment."

"What kind?"

"A land deal."

"You spent half the week in Mexico looking into a land deal?"

"It was a very big land deal, Mr. Posner. If it hadn't fallen through, it would have made me a fortune."

"Why didn't you tell us where you were going?" Arthur Spartling demanded.

I held my breath, hoping Jimmy's skill as a liar didn't flag at this critical juncture. The ice of his story was thinnest at this point. "Well," he said, looking somewhat abashed and ashamed, "for one thing I thought it was only going to take one day and since the day after the game was a day off anyway, I figured I could wrap the deal up on Tuesday and be back Wednesday for practice as usual. Another thing was, I wasn't sure you'd have approved of the man I was dealing with if I'd told you."

"Who was that?" Spartling inquired, leaning forward.

"Smiley Kruger."

The three interrogators made one face of distaste. Kruger was known to them as a bad apple. Arthur Spartling articulated that sentiment and Jimmy said, "I know. I knew it at the time but I thought his deal was for real. I owed it to myself to look into it, at least. If it came off, I'd have been fixed for life. But it didn't. I decided he was trying to hustle me so I turned his proposition down."

Well done, Jimmy. So far you've made it sound like nothing more than an indiscretion.

"That took all week?" pursued Spartling.

"No, sir. But you see, just as I was ready to head for home the papers came out with that story about me shaving points in the Detroit game and maybe killing that gambler."

"At that point you should have come home at once to clear your name," Spartling said pontifically.

"I know, I know, but I got scared. I called Dave and he advised me to stay down in Manzanillo as long as I could until he could figure out what was behind the removal of the game from the betting boards and the murder of that guy Negri."

Posner looked at me wrathfully. "Then you knew all the time where Jimmy was," he said with ominous calm.

"Guilty as charged, Your Honor," I said. "I thought it was in my client's best interest to stay put."

"The Commissioner will be overjoyed to hear it," Posner replied. He gazed at the back of his hand, looking like some Roman consul in the court of a vanquished king. "Well, Bolt, did you get to the bottom of it?"

"Not entirely but enough to satisfy me it had nothing to do with Jimmy. This Negri fella worked for a gambler named Sam Wisniak. Apparently, Negri thought he had some inside information about the Lion-Racer game and bet very heavily on it without telling his boss. Wisniak got rather indignant about that and had Negri killed. I still don't know what information Negri had or thought he had and I suspect we never will. But lookee here, if this boy had gone into the tank," I said, pointing my thumb at Jimmy, "he'd have managed to win the game inside the point spread or he'd have lost the game entirely. As it was, he whipped the Lions by a big margin. A quarterback who's in on a fix doesn't behave that way. Right or wrong?"

Posner glared, looking very frustrated and not completely convinced. "Then you're going to stick to the story that Jimmy's disappearance had nothing to do with Al Negri?"

"You want me to run through it again?" I said pee-vishly. "Unless and until you can produce evidence to the contrary, I'm going to stand behind Jimmy. And while I don't wish to tell you how to run your business, Mr. Posner, it strikes me that the Commission has no choice but to do the same. Unless, of course, you want Roy Lescade's smear to stand and stink forever and blight the name of professional football." I turned to Arthur Spartling and said, "Doesn't that make sense, Mr. Spartling?"

"Yes," he said with a funereal sigh, "I suppose that from a public relations viewpoint it does. But speaking personally, I don't buy it. I have no grounds for saying so but my gut reaction is that Jimmy is. . . has been less than candid with us. On the other hand, I have my team to think about. And the Commissioner," he addressed Posner, "has his league to think about. Reluctantly, Bolt, I have to agree with you, we have no choice but to back Jimmy up and come out with a strong denial." He looked thoughtfully at an airline route map on the wall of the lounge. "I wonder if there's some way we can put pressure on Roy Lescade to print an apology or retraction or something."

Jimmy and I traded looks. "An apology or retraction isn't going to be enough. People tend to remember the accusation and ignore the retraction."

Spartling nodded tacit agreement. "What'd you have in mind?"

"A libel suit."

That stirred Spartling up. "Not a bad idea. Except that Lescade never actually came out and said that Jimmy had consorted with this Negri fellow. He just printed specula-tions and innuendos. Jimmy is a public figure. He's fair game for speculations of that sort."

"Yes," I said, "but I think a lawyer could work up a

pretty fair case that Jimmy's reputation and the team's and the league's have been seriously damaged. And anyway, it's not important that we can win a suit. The important thing is bringing the action itself and bringing it with as much fanfare as we can create. The publicity surrounding it may offset the publicity created by Roy's original article. Maybe we can even force a settlement which we could play up as an admission that Roy had nothing concrete to base his article on."

I looked around and could tell I'd moved them in the direction I wanted to go. "Isn't Roy Lescade a close friend of yours?" Spartling asked.

"Yes, but this is an issue that goes higher than friendship."

There was a lapse of a minute while everyone thought about it, filling the room with heavy breathing. Hobie Gilmore sat chain-smoking. He hadn't said a thing and I wondered what he would say when he finally did.

At last, Posner said, "I'll have to discuss it with the Commissioner."

"Of course, you will," I said, just a little snidely.

Posner's eyes flashed a death ray at me. "I want to tell you something, Bolt, if we decide to back you up and this thing backfires, if it turns out that you two have been fucking us around, I'm going to shut you down so tight you'll be lucky to represent so much as a tiddlywinks player. It that clear?"

"Gotcha," I said, holding back a smile. I don't know why but this guy brought out the torturer in me.

We sat for a minute bathed in discomfort. The most that could be said of the decision we'd reached is that it was the least of evils. Spartling was dejected, Posner was livid, and Hobie Gilmore was absolutely appalled. Finally, Spartling looked at his watch, then at his coach. "You've got to get back to practice."

"Yeah," he grunted, getting to his feet.

Jimmy rose, too.

Hobie looked at him. "Don't bother."

"Huh?" Jimmy shifted his weight to one hip and looked questioningly at his coach.

"I said, don't bother. You're not starting tomorrow. For all I care, you don't even have to suit up tomorrow. I'm going with Gene, and if Gene is no good I'll bring in Ronnie and if Ronnie is no good, I'll quarterback myself. Plus, I'm fining you a thousand dollars."

Jimmy rocked on his heels and we all focused on Arthur Spartling. Spartling's jaw had plummeted and rested on two rolls of fat. He cleared his throat. "Hobie, you never said anything to me about this."

Hobie lit another cigarette and puffed frenetically. "I run this team, Mr. Spartling. That's my decision. No one goes AWOL on me and expects to get away with it, I don't care if he's Unitas and Namath rolled into one."

Spartling pounded the arm of his chair nervously. "But Hobie, this is a critical game coming up. We can't afford to go with our second- and third-string quarterbacks."

"Jimmy should have considered that before he chased down to Mexico to make his land deals," Gilmore spat out.

Jimmy looked to me for support but I wasn't sure it was my place to meddle. In fact, I tended to side with Hobie. Jimmy's jaunt to Mexico had undermined team spirit and discipline, had embarrassed Gilmore, disrupted routine, jeopardized the integrity of football—was he supposed to get off unpunished? I sat still as a stone, telling Jimmy with my eyes that this was his problem.

He looked pleadingly at Gilmore. "Coach, I absolutely agree with you. I deserve everything you can throw at me. You can have the fine. Hell, I'll play the rest of the season for free but don't keep me out of tomorrow's game, please."

"You'll start next week, but not tomorrow," he said, turning his back.

Jimmy held his hands out imploringly to Arthur Spartling. Spartling looked apoplectic. "Hobie," he said, addressing Gilmore's back, "we've got to go with our best shot tomorrow. There aren't that many games left. We blow our lead tomorrow, we may never recover. I've got my franchise to think about. We put a team in the playoffs, we're on the map. Don't make me give you a direct order. I've never told you how to run your football team, but this time—"

Gilmore whirled around, dropped his cigarette on the white linoleum and crushed it. "I'll play Jimmy tomorrow," he said. We were just about to draw big lungsful of relief when he added, "But that will be my last act as coach of the Indianapolis Racers."

I whistled quietly. Jimmy put his hands over his face. Barry Posner crossed his legs, which for him was a violent display of emotion. Spartling looked close to tears. Then he pulled himself together and said, "Gentlemen, I wonder if you could excuse us. I'd like to discuss this with Hobie privately."

I got up and motioned to Jimmy. We moved toward the door but Posner remained in his seat. "I'd like to be in on this, Mr. Spartling."

"This is none of your business, Posner," the peppery coach snapped.

"It's very much NFL business," Posner retorted, unintimidated. "Coming on top of Jimmy's disappearance and Roy Lescade's article, Jimmy's failure to start tomorrow or your resignation would certainly have an aggravating effect on the situation. I think the Commissioner must be represented in this conversation. And," he said, modifying his voice to a gentleness that was the closest thing to human I'd seen in Barry

Posner yet, "perhaps I can suggest some ways we can work out these differences." I'm not sure why Posner looked at me when he said this but there was something almost friendly, almost conspiratorial, in his glance. Suddenly I thought I understood and I nodded at him. I had a flash of insight into the kind of friendly persuasion Posner was going to bring to bear on these two. Hell, I'd experienced enough of it from him myself. With a hint here and a hint there, Posner could instill tremendous anxieties in both men, could probably scare them both half to death with "suggestions" that Hobie might have a tough time finding another coaching position around the league, that Spartling might find himself in bad grace with the Commissioner, which is not a good place for an owner to be.

I nudged Jimmy and said, "Let's go, son. Things are gonna work out okay."

I put my hand on the doorknob, then remembered something. "Say, Posner, didn't you and I have a deal?"

"A deal?"

"Forgotten already? You promised that if I produced Jimmy before tomorrow, you'd help me make the government drop its case against Bob Rubin."

He nodded stoically. "I did, didn't I?"

"Uh-huh."

"Well, if I did, I did. You're certainly not going to win any popularity contests with the Commissioner when all this is over."

"You're right about that. But if I may make a kindly suggestion. . .?"

"Yes?"

"Best not enter any popularity contests yourself, Posner."

"I'll make a note of that," he answered, sarcastically.

I pivoted on my heel and opened the lounge door. A tremendous babble went up and I shut it again quickly, forcing it closed against half a dozen shoulders thrusting it from the other side. "Uh-oh. The press are here."

Posner got up and walked past me to the door and pulled it open sharply. Four microphones were thrust under his chin, flashbulbs went off, and a roar of questions went up. The little guy stood there bravely with his hands up, looking like King Canute commanding the waves to be still. After a moment the shouting died down and he said, "Gentlemen, I'll have a statement for you in half an hour. That's all I have to say for the moment." He looked at me and said, "How's your blocking?"

I in turn looked at Jimmy, who'd shrunk behind a chair, looking terrified. "Jimmy-boy. . . quarterback draw on three." He stepped behind me as the uproar outside started all over again. I put my forearm in front of my face to protect it against microphones and cameras. "Hut!" I barked. "Hut! Hut!" Then I plunged into the crowd head-first, Jimmy clutching my coattails.

Chapter XV

• • • •

And so it came to pass that Jimmy Quinn did start after all for the Indianapolis Racers against the Green Bay Packers.

Right up to the opening kickoff, I cherished the fantasy that despite a five-day layoff, a couple hours' practice Saturday following a sleepless night and five-hour flight and the ordeal at the airport, and a light workout Sunday morning, Jimmy would come in cold and still blow the Packers out of the stadium. That's a nice Hollywood ending but it doesn't take into account the realities of athletic conditioning—or of the Green Bay defensive unit. Jimmy's head was still in Manzanillo. He didn't have time to learn the new plays Coach Gilmore had inserted into the book to offset the Packers' brutal rush and gainsay its complicated pass defense, which seemed to flip-flop from zone to man-to-man completely at random. The Racers were lucky to hang any numbers at all on the scoreboard—17 of them, thanks to luck more than skill—and to hold the Packers to 34.

The only good thing to come out of the game was that Jimmy's teammates were buoyed by his return and felt confident they could clinch a playoff berth next week despite the loss of a game lead in the standings.

The press and media were there at division strength
and hounded Jimmy, Hobie Gilmore, and Arthur Spartling
mercilessly. They were not content with the statement Barry
Posner had issued at the airport the day before—I could
scarcely blame them—but they ran up against a solid wall
of No Comments and had to satisfy themselves with their
speculations. These would soon be put into their proper perspective by the libel suit we launched the following week.

As it happened, I read about the game in the papers. I hadn't
hung around to see the debacle at Racer stadium but flew back
to New York Saturday night and put in a solitary morning at the
office on Sunday. I'd neglected things at the office atrociously
and wanted to clear a ton of work away without phone interrup-
tions. Tomorrow the phones would be jangling off their cradles;
today my office was like a tomb. In more ways than one, too,
because there was no heat in the building on Sunday and I
damn near froze my ass off. In scarf and gloves, I pored over
the office log, memos, correspondence, revenue flow ledgers
and petty cash chits, thanking my stars for a couple of aides
who'd become as compulsive about order as I.

It hadn't always been thus. Trish and Dennis had been
jealous rivals when Dennis first joined the firm. Each had
tried to outdo each other to impress me but by concentrating
on the more glamorous aspects of the business they'd disdained to dirty their hands with the more routine functions.
The victim of this childish competition had been office
routine. I'd come back from a trip once to find a week's
filing unfiled, checks undeposited, letters unanswered,
messages unreturned, and nothing settled but a layer of
dust over the paperwork. Plus, some hideous purple stains
on carpet and upholstery where a temporary secretary had
spilled prune whip yogurt. So, I'd read them the riot act
and now they were both super-organized neatniks.

One item in Trish's memo engaged my attention particularly. It was a report on the status of her preliminary discussions with Gary Albert, general manager of the New York Jets, about hiring Bob Rubin. As expected, Albert had said he could not begin negotiations for Rubin because of the pending government action against him. Trish had asked him what he would offer if Rubin did, somehow, beat the federal rap. Albert had named a sum that was rather modest but which I did not think too far out of line. Trish had laughed in his face and named a figure three times higher, which had understandably miffed Albert. They were to resume discussions tomorrow morning—discussions predicated, of course, on Bob Rubin being free to play.

I was tempted to call Trish and talk the situation over. It struck me that her involvement with Rubin had clouded her judgment. No doubt her enthusiasm for him had made her price her client out of the market—I don't care how good he was, he was not worth the money she was asking. I'd seen Gary Albert walk away from negotiations and not come back just to teach greedy agents a lesson. It could happen here.

Yet I didn't want to meddle. Trish was extremely competent and extremely proud. To intercede would not only hurt her feelings but undercut her authority. Owners might feel that if they didn't reach terms with Trish, they could always turn to me. I had to stand behind her. But the rest of the day I thought long and hard about some way to modify her demands before she blew the negotiations sky-high.

I cleared away a mountain of material, penned decisions on memos, and extracted a short list of phone calls requiring my personal attention. I called Las Hadas in Manzanillo and arranged for them to put my luggage on an airplane. Then I went home and watched football on television. The phone rang a number of times and I ignored it. This was the first quiet moment I'd had in a week, and whatever it was could wait for the outcome of the Dallas-Giants game on CBS—the Green Bay-Racers game wasn't on—followed by the Oakland-Kansas City game on NBC. I had not lived long enough in New York City to become a Giants fan and probably never would. I savored the deep satisfaction of watching the Cowboys walk over the Giants. Kansas City upset Oakland in a skin-of-the-teeth thriller that left me limp but deliciously content. Some people get off on sex, some on dope, some on work, some on dancing and mountain-climbing. I get off watching sports on television. I long ago made peace with myself over this aberration.

The phone sounded as I was stepping out of the shower, leaving behind a final layer of Mexican dust mingled with a gallon or so of nervous perspiration. I felt capable once more of facing the outside world and lifted my blackout on phone communications.

"Bolt?"

"Yo?"

"Barry Posner."

"A very good day to you, sir," I said with an Elizabethan flourish.

As usual, Posner sliced through pleasantries to the heart of his business. "You have an appointment to-morrow afternoon at one with a Presidential assistant named Nat Altshuler."

"To discuss Bob Rubin, you mean?"

"You can discuss the oil depletion allowance with him for all I care."

"Thanks. At least tell me if he's predisposed in Rubin's favor."

"His mind is open."

"Did you at least put in a good word for Rubin?"

"Come on, Bolt, does that sound like me?"

"Sorry. I thought maybe you'd had a religious conversion experience since yesterday."

"You're supposed to meet Altshuler on the third floor of the Old Senate Office Building, Room 307. I've kept my bargain with you, but from here on in, you're on your own."

"May the good Lord bless and keep you," I said. Mostly keep you, I added silently, returning the phone to its cradle.

I hung over the phone a moment, then dialed Trish. Her voice was slightly slurred when she picked up. "Ullo."

"Trish? Dave."

"Oh, hi."

"Were you sleeping?"

"No, making love."

I gulped. "Oh. Uh, I can call back."

"No, that's all right. Just a second." She put the phone down, leaving me free to exercise my imagination about what she had to do during the minute she was away. "There," she said brightly when she came back on. "How's your face?"

"My face?"

"No new lumps on it? I thought for sure you'd bring some home from Mexico. Anyhow, nice going on the Jimmy Quinn affair. Can't wait to hear the inside poop on that one. What's up?"

"I've a date to discuss Bob Rubin's case with a Presidential aide tomorrow afternoon."

"Oh, you bubby!"

The hairs on the back of my neck prickled. Trish called me bubby whenever I performed some extraordinary favor for her. The word, according to her, derives from a Yiddish term of endearment, bubeleh, but of all the New Yorkisms I have to suffer, "bubby" ranks highest on my shit list. Nothing is better calculated to make me an anti-Semite than calling me "bubby." I brooded a few seconds while she covered the phone and relayed the information to Bob Rubin lying next to her in bed.

"Tell me which plane you're taking and I'll arrange for Gartha Wilcoxon to join you," Trish said.

"Gartha Wilcoxon? What the hell do I need her for?"

"Well, hell, Dave, you wouldn't think of going to Washington without Bob's attorney, would you?"

"As a matter of fact, I would. I don't think a see-through peasant blouse or a spangled pants-suit will exactly help our case."

Trish laughed. "Don't worry, she knows how to dress for these occasions. Don't underestimate her. She's a very smart cookie."

"So everyone keeps telling me. All right, I'll make a deal with you. If you'll let me be present for your discussions with the Jets tomorrow morning, I'll let Gartha come with me tomorrow afternoon."

Her voice turned a little defensive. "Why do you want to do that?"

I couldn't tell her I was afraid she was botching the negotiations. "I may have some suggestions to contribute," I said neutrally.

"Don't you think I'm doing a good job?"

"You're doing a terrific job. But my invitation to Washington puts things in a new light. I'd like to throw it into the hopper tomorrow when you meet with Gary Albert."

She thought about it a few seconds. "We're having breakfast at the Algonquin tomorrow morning at eight."

"How come you're not meeting Gary at 595 Madison?" That was the Jets' headquarters.

"Because he can shout at 595 Madison. He can't in a public restaurant and certainly not in the Algonquin!"

"You're a pretty smart cookie yourself," I said. "See you tomorrow morning."

I had some second thoughts about Trish's smarts as I stepped into the fusty elegance of the Algonquin Hotel on 44th Street off Sixth Avenue (I'd become enough of a New Yorker not to call it Avenue of the Americas). The Algonquin was at one time the stamping ground for New York's literary set and was still used for editorial lunches by many people in the publishing world. I'd been there on numerous occasions to discuss book deals for some of my clients and had always come away feeling I'd spent two hours in a clean, well-lighted crypt. But this morning, the subdued tinkle of silver on fine china was counterpointed by the sharp, loud, and angry voice of Gary Albert, general manager of the New York Jets. Trish's gambit had apparently not been as successful as she'd hoped. Albert wasn't quite making a scene, but neither was he intimidated by the muted propriety of this hallowed old dining room.

". . . don't care if he rushes eighteen hundred yards a game," Albert was saying, "he's not worth a hundred thousand a year to us. Not yet, at any rate." Half the diners in the room were either staring or leaning in the direction of Trish's table, listening, and the maître d' was making fussy gestures with his hands in an attempt to get Albert to lower his voice. I strode into the room and Albert saw me. "Ah, Dave, thank God!"

Gary was a slim, dark-complected, youthful-looking man in his early forties, well dressed in a bright blue blazer and sea-green tie. Trish was dressed in a variety of mixed and matched wools and was glaring at Albert with a piece of bacon impaled on the tines of her fork.

"Good morning. What seems to be the problem?" I motioned to our waiter for a cup of coffee.

"Dave, don't get me wrong, I'm head over heels in love with this lady," Gary said, patting Trish's free hand, "but her notions about Bob Rubin's value to us or to any other team in the NFL are sadly overinflated."

It was good strategy to come immediately to Trish's aid. "Oh, I don't know, Gary," I said, breaking off a breadstick and dipping it into a pat of butter. "Maybe your notions are underinflated."

Albert groaned. "Look, I admit the guy is good, but the Canadian Football League is not the National Football League. The quality of play there—"

"That's a questionable assumption," I said.

Albert shook his head. "Do you know how much talent I can buy for a hundred thousand dollars a year?"

I shrugged. "Buy it. Buy five rookie running backs with it. And when Emerson Boozer retires, you use those rookies, by all means. Maybe they'll gain a thousand yards for you, combined. Maybe."

Albert shook his head again, this time in big bearish sweeps. "Christ, if I'd known you were going to support Trish's ridiculous demands this morning, I wouldn't have bothered coming."

"I don't tell Trish what to do, Gary. If she thinks Bob Rubin is worth a hundred thou a year—"

"And don't forget the hundred thou bonus," Trish interjected.

"Yes. If she thinks Bob Rubin is worth that price, that's good enough for me. We're giving you first crack at him but the Jets aren't the only team in the league."

"I'm authorized to offer you a twenty-five-thousand-dollar bonus, thirty thousand a year for three years, and I'll pick up the tab for breakfast. That's the best I can do." He searched the room for the waiter.

"Unacceptable, including picking up the tab for breakfast," I said, catching the waiter's eye and making a scribbling gesture for the check.

Albert sipped some coffee, then sighed. "It's probably all irrelevant, anyway, since it's all predicated on Rubin's beating the federal rap, which I suspect he isn't going to do."

"I have a date to see a man in the White House about that this afternoon," I said.

Albert raised an eyebrow. "Think you can do anything?"

"I have one or two ideas on that score. In fact, I have a minor brainstorm on that score."

They both leaned forward. "You didn't tell me," Trish said.

"It came to me last night."

Trish looked at me expectantly. "Well?"

"I can't tell you yet. But I can tell you this: if it works, it will render the question of Bob's salary superfluous. So don't go away, Gary—we may be able to do business yet."

I found Gartha Wilcoxon standing near the Eastern departures gate at LaGuardia and it was hard to believe this was the same girl who'd been dressed in studded jeans the first time I'd met her. She wore a modest black suit with a flared skirt over a white blouse, with just a couple of bangles on her wrist and a silver medallion shaped like a dove over her bosom. Her hair had been teased out of its tight cornrows by some arcane process and was now fluffed into a natural of conservative height. Her makeup was understated and she carried a sensible black attaché case and an unobtrusive shoulder bag. There was nothing faintly resembling a nail head anywhere on her ensemble. She looked like nothing more radical than an Avon lady.

On the flight down to Washington, she told me all about herself. Except for her color, she was not atypical of countless sons and daughters of upper middle-class homes, sons and daughters who'd entered young maturity in the late 1960s. Her folks had made a lot of money in Atlanta real estate and sent her to Columbia University. There she'd been polarized to the far left by the Vietnam war and had participated in the protest movement, though she fell short of occupying the Dean's office or pouring chicken blood on draft board files. Her parents had imbued her with a mission: to enter the legal profession. Had she gotten into trouble, that would have been the end of her hopes for law school. But she'd carried some radicalism with her to Columbia Law School and though it had been muted since then by the conservative tradition of the profession, it had by no means been extinguished. Gartha Wilcoxon had learned to play ball with the Establishment but not entirely. After graduation, she'd found herself with lots of job offers and no end of causes for which a black female lawyer was precisely the right thing. She was a good lawyer, a good black, and, I was beginning to think, a good female.

She showed me a statement she'd prepared and I told her my scheme for inducing the government to drop its case against Bob Rubin. Between us, we'd come up with the strongest possible attack and by the time we stepped off the plane in Washington, I'd begun to feel genuinely hopeful. We went over the plan one final time in a hamburger shop at the airport, then caught a cab into the District of Columbia. We got out at the Old Senate Office Building. A security guard made Gartha open her attaché case, then passed us through to a grand vaulted chamber where an exhibition of American combat medals and decorations was on display in glass cases around the marbled walls and pillars. We took an elevator to the third floor and walked with hollow clacking footsteps past the offices of senators from New York, Rhode Island, New Jersey, Michigan, and Massachusetts.

About halfway down the corridor, we stopped in front of a door marked "Subcommittee on Foreign Relations." Descending from it on brass chains was another sign that said "Not in Session." I turned a large brass knob and the oaken door swung open. We stepped into a large paneled room hung with dark, gilt-framed portraits. In the center stood a huge rosewood table surrounded by twenty chairs of walnut and red leather. A visitors' gallery sloped up to a portrait-filled wall. "Jesus," whistled Gartha, "is this a meeting or a state function?"

"Just a meeting," answered a deep voice from the visitors' gallery. I looked over there and saw a bald man slumped in the front row with his feet slung over the rail. This was Nat Altshuler. He stretched noisily and got to his feet. He was unusually tall and lean, expensively dressed and swarthily tanned. He slid out of the gallery, extending his hand with an engaging smile. "Sorry, I was grabbing a nap. In my job, you sleep when and where you can. You must be Dave Bolt, and this. . .?"

"Gartha Wilcoxon, Mr. Rubin's attorney," my companion introduced herself. I noticed the defensiveness in her voice, but Altshuler, a trained diplomat obviously, didn't evince so much as a twitch of surprise.

"We can sit here and all feel enormously intimidated, or go into the adjoining lounge, which you'll probably find cozier," Altshuler said, leading us into a room which was smaller but scarcely less imposing, richly paneled and wainscoted, filled with leather armchairs and antiques and portraits. He flipped on the lights, opened a cupboard and began spooning coffee out of a Savarin can into the basket of an electric coffee pot, chatting garrulously about Washington life, segueing easily into sports and then Canadian football and then American football and then Bob Rubin.

He was extremely adept at putting people at their ease but I sat on the edge of my chair forcing myself to remain alert. Talkative people can lull you off your guard and zing you before you know you've been zung.

His monologue extended through the pouring of our coffee. He produced a pint of cream from a tiny refrigerator and a box of sugar cubes from the pantry and stopped talking only long enough to sip his coffee. For a moment he fell into a trancelike silence. Then he said, "The President is personally interested in the case of Bob Rubin. He wants to make an example of him but he's not sure what kind of example. Vietnam still hangs over Washington like a poison cloud. The conclusion of our involvement there has by no means signaled the conclusion of our sensitivity over the disaster. If anything, it's intensified it. It's hard to say which way the cat—I mean the President, of course—will jump on the question of Rubin. But he does see Rubin as an opportunity to do something, to say something to the country. He's open to your suggestions."

"We have some," Gartha said.

He seemed disinclined to entertain them just yet. Instead, he lectured Gartha. "Your client had ample opportunity to take advantage of the clemency program established by the President in September 1974. He did not. Now he wants to come back into the country but the clemency program expired in the spring of 1975 and there is no longer any formal machinery for him to use, except the Constitutional one of Presidential pardon or the informal one of political negotiation. I hardly think the President will take the first course—as you may know, he's a little choosy about the people he pardons." He smiled at his own little joke.

"We expected that," Gartha said. "But we know that where there's a will there's a political way."

"That cuts both ways, my dear. Your client has to have the will, too. From what I know and have read about him, he's somewhat pigheaded. He refuses to compromise the least bit. If he remains intransigent, we'll have nothing to say to him or do with him. We might be willing to meet him halfway but not more than halfway. That would make a mockery of all we did in Vietnam. Never mind that Vietnam was a mockery in itself," he added hastily to ward off the obvious rejoinder. "The sacrifices American boys made in that country were not. It would be politically as well as morally inappropriate for the President to let Bob Rubin rub our faces in our mistakes. Some sort of apology, some expression of his desire to make amends, is in order."

"We recognize that, Mr. Altshuler," I said. "And we have a concrete proposal that I think you'll find a firm basis for a settlement."

"I'm listening."

Gartha opened her attaché case. "Mr. Altshuler, I've framed the text of an apology," she said, drawing out the text she'd showed me on the plane. I'd been most impressed by it. It was beautifully phrased and had the political virtue of saying something and nothing at the same time. It reminded me of those apologies offered to save the honor of men about to engage in a duel. It said in effect, "I don't regret what I did but I'm sorry for the difficulties I've created."

Altshuler studied it, pursing his lips and nodding approvingly. He looked at Gartha. "You're a clever young lady. We might be able to live with this. But it doesn't answer the question of what we are to do with your man. Even if the clemency program still existed, playing football was not one of the options offered to draft evaders and deserters seeking amnesty. There was the Peace Corps, hospital work, that sort of thing. One can argue, and it will be argued, that for Bob

Rubin, playing football is hardly a form of punishment. It's simply not—how may I put it—sacrificial enough."

It was now time for me to come forward with my proposed solution. I'd tossed in my bed last night for hours probing for an answer and oddly enough it had come to me only after I'd dropped my quest for it and permitted my mind to drift back over my recent adventures with another client, Jimmy Quinn. In our meeting at the airport with Barry Posner, Arthur Spartling, and Hobie Gilmore, Jimmy had said something about not caring whether he played out the rest of the season for no salary at all, as long as he could play. I'd jumped out of bed as this idea crossed circuits with the problem of Bob Rubin and I paced the bedroom excitedly, honing the idea to a sharp edge.

"Would you consider Bob's salary sacrifice enough?" I posed to Altshuler.

He grasped it at once. "You mean, he would turn his income over to charity or something?"

"Yes, but particularly some Vietnam-identified charity, war orphans or refugees or something like that."

He tried to cloak his interest behind those well-composed eyes but I could see he was rapidly tracing the effects of our offer down its political byways. "It would have to be well publicized," he said to himself, aloud.

Gartha picked up his drift. "That goes without saying, Mr. Altshuler. You see, sir, the President's amnesty program was not particularly successful—only a small percentage of men applied out of the many who were eligible. I think one reason was, the program didn't have high enough visibility. I mean, you didn't have someone singled out to symbolize the government's compassion. Now, you have Bob Rubin. Every time he took the field to play football, the public would see that symbol and would be reminded. He would be a living tribute to the President's healing influence."

"Yes, yes, I can see it," he said heatedly. Then he turned to me. "I would imagine you're prepared to give up your commission to charity, too?"

I almost fell off my chair. "Well, uh. . ." I gasped and stammered. "I never really thought about it. But I. . . uh. . . suppose. . ."

Suddenly Altshuler broke into hearty laughter, slapping me jovially on the knee. "Sorry, Bolt, just my idea of a joke. I wanted to see your face. It was beautiful. I wish I'd had a camera."

I laughed sheepishly. "Well, what the hell, Mr. Altshuler, I will contribute my commission to charity! Might as well score a little public relations coup for myself while I'm at it."

He raised a finger. "Don't be too impulsive. Bob Rubin gives up his salary, he looks like a hero. You give up your commission, you'll probably look like a fool. More coffee?"

I covered my cup but Gartha held hers out for a refill. "How fast could we move on this thing?" she asked.

He chuckled. "You haven't much experience of Washington or you wouldn't ask that question. But actually, the Attorney General has been talking about a swift prosecution so I might be able to hammer something out for you rather quickly. Just bear in mind what I said before, the legal machinery for clemency has expired so we're at a disadvantage in not having a strong framework to hang this thing on. But I've no doubt the right strings can be pulled if the President buys your solution. Yes, you're a very clever young lady, Ms. Wilcoxon. How would you like to work for the government?"

The question came like a thunderbolt and rattled poor Gartha's cup, splashing droplets of coffee on her skirt. She quickly regained her composure. "I'm very flattered, Mr. Altshuler—but I don't think so. Less than ten years ago, I was picketing the White House and shouting some extremely obscene things at National Guardsmen. I've mellowed a little since those days but I don't think I'd ever feel too comfortable working in the same wonderful town that gave us Vietnam and Watergate."

He smiled gently. "If we'd had more people like you in the government, we might not have had Vietnam and Watergate."

"You got any jobs open for me, while you're at it?" I said lightly.

He pondered my question a moment. "Our Costa Rican embassy needs a busboy."

"Well, if it's all the same to you, sir. . ." I said.

Chapter XVI

· · · ·

For every host, there comes a moment at his party when the function is wound up and running by itself. The guests are well oiled and the food moving like at a Polish wedding and the decibels have reached the elevated subway level. You've observed all the formalities, the greetings and the introductions and the small talk. Now you can step away and preside, anonymously, invisibly, over the affair, congratulating yourself smugly.

This describes the contented feeling that settled (with two drinks for lubricant) over my soul as I leaned against the doorjamb between kitchen and living room surveying the throng of guests come to celebrate Bob Rubin's signing with the New York Jets. Word of the negotiated compromise with the government had come down yesterday morning in time for Roy Lescade to break the story exclusively in the Post. Though sports headlines traditionally occupy the back page of that paper, this one grabbed the front page. It carried far more weight than the average sports story, bearing significant implications for some hundred thousand young men, their parents and girls and wives and kids, all still caught in the teeth of the Vietnam war. I exulted. One more national wound healed and I'd helped to make it so.

I'd had to laugh when I saw that headline, though. Because as big as Roy had played up the Bob Rubin story, he'd played down the story of Jimmy Quinn's reappearance on the Indianapolis roster, Now, that story had made front-page news just about everywhere else in the country, including New York's morning newspapers, the Times and the News. But Roy had given it three lines and buried it in the early edition, along with several pounds of egg he'd had to scrape off his face. Nor was the Post exactly devoting banner headlines to the lawsuit Jimmy'd brought against it and against Roy, whereas the rest of the New York media were having a field day with it, roundly panning Roy for his rare error of judgment. "Roy Lescade doesn't boot the ball often," Dave Anderson wrote in the Times, "but when he does it's in the seventh game of the World Series."

I looked around the room and found Roy in a corner talking to Gary Albert of the Jets. Roy's suit looked like it had been used to cover Aunt Minnie's compost heap, and his elbow was bent at its customary forty-five-degree angle to accommodate a generous glassful of Wild Turkey. He assiduously avoided my glance. Gary Albert was all grins, of course. We'd given him Bob Rubin for a thirty-five-thousand-dollar bonus and thirty-five thousand a year for two years, very close to what he'd offered and considerably less than Trish had been demanding. This we were able to do with complete salvation of face since every penny of it (less our commission, which on Nat Altshuler's advice, we'd decided to keep) went to charity anyway. If Bob Rubin performed as expected, we'd nail the Jets two years from now when the contract came up for renewal and Bob's obligation to the government terminated.

Back to back with Albert was Bob Rubin rapping ani-
matedly with Gartha Wilcoxon while a knot of reporters
scribbled down every word. Bob's expression was that of a
prisoner whose firing squad had inadvertently loaded up with
blank cartridges. He literally seemed six inches taller than I'd
remembered him probably because his feet weren't touching
the ground today. In a corner of the room, his parents and kid
sister looked on with eyes glazed with happiness.

Gartha had undergone another of her amazing trans-
formations. She'd donned velvet pants and a printed
chiffon blouse that might as well have been a tattoo for all
it concealed of her high, small breasts and plum-colored
nipples. Her hair was braided in some complicated pretzel
coif and shot through with long silver pins to hold it together. I hadn't been kidding when I'd told Nat Altshuler
I was interested in Gartha for myself. I wasn't sure how I
might work her into my operation but this kid was loaded
with charm, talent, and intelligence, and I'd find a way to
employ them to further my fortunes.

And there was Trish.

Trish was as ripe with pride as a watermelon, flitting
around my apartment in a white silk hostess jump-suit slit
up the thighs to her pelvis. There should have been panties
somewhere around that part of her anatomy, but I spied
none, and goddamn, I tried, believe me. It was odd how,
familiar to me as she was, I still ogled her like a stranger.
I'm ashamed to admit it but I longed for her to pass in front
of the spotlight illuminating my house plants so that I could
see the outline of her crotch.

As if picking up these lusty vibrations, Trish looked up,
licked her lips, and flowed over to me. "Like it? Halston,
three hundred dollars."

"Put it on my bill."

"You sound like a husband."

"You spend like a wife."

"For this occasion, it's worth it."

"For sure. You deserve all the credit."

"No, that goes to Gartha. And to you. At least, once you budged your ass to help Bob."

"You gonna marry him?"

"Are you gonna marry me?"

"I don't think so."

"Well, then, maybe I'll marry him."

"If you marry him, I won't let you represent him. Conflict of interest and all that."

She glared at me. "You know, you're a real swine. But I do love you."

We stood together watching the party, feeling close to one another though events had wedged us farther apart than ever, emotionally speaking. There'd come a point in our relationship when we knew we'd never sleep together, now, we'd reached the point where we'd probably never marry. Perhaps one day we'd reach the point where we went our separate ways entirely. Just a glimpse of that possibility had scared the bejesus out of me. I'd always have her resignation note on my desk to remind me never to take her for granted. I reached down, found Trish's warm hand, and squeezed it. She clutched me tightly a minute, then abruptly pecked me on the cheek with her perfumed mouth and whisked away in her Halston to recapture Bob Rubin from Gartha.

Roy Lescade observed that I was free and disengaged from Gary Albert. He ambled over, heeled forward as if chasing the drink he held in front of his nose.

"Hullo, Dave."

"What, no Polack jokes today?"

"Not for you."

"Why so glum?"

"You know fucking-A well why, shit-ass."

"Oh, you mean that l'il ol' libel suit?"

"That li'l ol' million-dollar libel suit, you mean."

"Look at the bright side. It could have been for five million."

"We are not amused. I happen to know you put Jimmy Quinn up to it. I also happen to suspect the Racers and maybe even the NFL are financing it."

"I can't say one way or the other about the latter but I freely confess to the former. But it ain't as if I didn't warn you, Roy. You got no one to blame but yourself. You based your story on hearsay and half-baked detective work. You went off half-cocked just to get even with me for screwing you out of a story once upon a time. Very poor journalism, Roy, not up to your customary mark."

He leaned closer, enveloping my face in an alcoholic smog. "Now, lookee here, Dave, you know and I know goddamn good and well that Jimmy Quinn put in for a fix before the Detroit game."

"All circumstantial, buddy, all circumstantial. You've got a lot of pieces but you put 'em together too hastily. If you'd asked me, I'd have told you to try putting 'em together another way. You'd have gotten a totally different picture and you wouldn't be the laughingstock of your profession this afternoon."

"I suppose you're right," he sighed. Then a funny twinkle came into his eyes, one I liked very little. "But I'm just wondering, Dave. . ."

"What's that?"

"Who's gonna look like a laughingstock when I have Ladrue Retting take the stand? And Ricky Lindner? And Shorty LeBrun? And Carl Janeway? And Buddy Esterbrook and the other players who invested with Jimmy?"

A shock wave ripped through me and I wasn't sure my

knees would support me. "How do you know about them?"

"A little bird told me, guy by the name of Smiley Kruger. Called me from Mexico and told me the whole story."

"That miserable fuck!" I muttered, and I just happened to say it during one of those incomprehensible lulls that occur randomly at a party. Everyone turned and stared. I pushed Roy into the kitchen.

"'Very poor journalism, Roy. Not up to your customary mark,'" he quoted back to me, laughing maliciously.

"I'll kill that sonofabitch," I said, pounding my kitchen counter. Then, feebly, I said, "You still have no proof."

"No, but do you really believe every one of those guys is gonna keep his mouth shut when our attorneys start putting the screws on them in court? It's all gonna come out, Dave, the crazy Australian land scheme, Jimmy's attempt to repay his friends by shaving points for Al Negri—your suppression of that list. We're gonna rip your ass, Dave and I'll see to it that this is the best-publicized courtroom drama since the trial of Sir Thomas More. Now, think of all that ballyhoo, Dave. Think of all that shit smeared on Jimmy and the league and on you."

"Would you really do that?"

"I'm about to. On the other hand, it would be a great pity. Like they say, the only ones who profit from lawsuits are the lawyers. But I'd be willing to file what Kruger told me in the trash basket of my mind if you're willing to drop the suit. What say?"

I took a deep breath and expelled it with a woeful groan. "All right. I'll talk to my lawyer right after the party."

"Does this mean we're friends again?"

We looked at each other like mortal adversaries in a war that had just been declared finished. "Fuck yes!" I said, embracing him like a brother.

He pushed open the kitchen door and surveyed the party. "Christ, don't that colored lawyer-gal have the smartest little titties, though?" he whistled. "Think she might like to change her luck?"

I slapped him on the shoulder. "Roy, I'd say your chances with her are about as good as my discovering a major oil field under my crapper."

"You never can tell," he said, tilting in the direction of Gartha Wilcoxon.

I stayed in the kitchen, picked up the phone, and dialed Jimmy Quinn's number in Indianapolis. Jimmy picked it up on the first ring. I'd told him to stand by for the news of a possible settlement. We'd reached one. Only, it was not the one I'd bargained for.

"Bad news, Jimmy. Roy Lescade found out about the Suicide Squad."

There was a stunned silence. "Who told him?"

"Can't you guess?"

"Smiley Kruger." He murmured an oath. "What are you going to do?"

"We have no choice." I told him the deal I'd struck with Roy. "I'm sorry. But look at it this way. Just by bringing the suit, we've restored your credibility, which is all we ever hoped to do anyway."

"Yeah. But all that money…"

"You're still ahead with what you made off Smiley Kruger. And you still have an opportunity to make a killing."

"I do? How's that?"

"Take your team to the playoffs."

He laughed bitterly. "Yeah, but I've got to work for that money."

"You don't call the last couple of weeks work?"

"You're right. Dave, I'm sorry as hell about all of this."

"Well, what can I say?"

There was an abashed pause. Then, "Carol wants to thank you. Hold on."

My heart began to triphammer but before I could compose myself she was on the line, saying as much as she could safely say. "You've been wonderful to us."

"How're you two getting along?" I asked.

"Much, much better, thanks to you."

"He doesn't, um. . ."

"No," she said neutrally as if we were discussing the weather.

"He just suspects a little, I reckon?"

"Uh-huh."

"Well, good. Maybe he won't take you for granted anymore."

"Let's hope so," she said guardedly.

"I'm only sorry that. . ."

"Yes, me too," she said. It's amazing how much lovers can convey using this kind of code. "Well, goodbye, Dave. Maybe we'll see you soon if we make the playoffs. A win next week and we clinch, you know."

"I'll rub my lucky charm."

"Oh—and there's someone else here who wants to speak to you."

There was a fumbling of the phone and some parental prompting. Then: "Uncle Dave?" It was little Emily.

"Hi, sweetheart."

"When are you coming back? My doll's head came off."

"Your daddy's home now. He can do it, you don't need me."

"But I like you."

"I like you, too, darlin'," I said, nervously hoping she wouldn't ask me when we were all going to a motel again.

"Can we get married?"

"Best proposition I've heard in weeks. Ask me again in eighteen years," I said, blowing her a goodbye kiss, hanging up gently and returning to my party.

If You Liked The Pro Series, You Might Like: Fightcard: Three Punch Combo

Veteran LAPD detective and bestselling author Paul Bishop puts up his dukes to deliver a trio of knockout stories in Three Punch Combo.

Intimately familiar with the mean streets of Los Angeles and the unforgiving brutality of the boxing ring, Bishop's insider knowledge drags readers into a world where most fear to tread.

Bishop's many novels, including the bestselling Lie Catchers, are consistently praised for their uncanny realism and lyrical prose—traits again on full display in Three Punch Combo.

AVAILABLE NOW ON AMAZON

About the Author

Though Richard Curtis is best known as a leading New York literary agent, he is also author of dozens of works of fiction and nonfiction published by leading publishers, as well as numerous works of humor and award-winning satire. His plays have been performed in numerous venues and festivals in New York. He is currently writing, producing and directing The Creepery, a series of horror podcasts scheduled for launch late in 2020.

Curtis's interest in emerging media and technology led to his founding of the first commercial e-book publishing company in the English language seven years before the introduction of the Kindle and the Digital Revolution.

Curtis was the first president of the Independent Literary Agents Association and was President of the Association of Authors' Representatives in 1996 and 1997.

Early in his freelance career he conceived The Pro, featuring a sports agent sleuth and action hero (modeled after Dallas Cowboys quarterback Don Meredith). Unlike his book's hero, Curtis is not very good with his fists.